The Shadow World

Jane Johnson

Illustrated by Adam Stower

D1422599

SIMON AND SCHUSTER

SIMON AND SCHUSTER
First published in Great Britain in 2006 by Simon & Schuster UK Ltd
A Viacom company

1 3 5 7 9 10 8 6 4 2

Simon & Schuster UK Ltd
Africa House
64-78 Kingsway
London WC2B 6AH

A CIP catalogue record for this book is available from the British Library

ISBN 0 689 86082 X

Typeset in Garamond by M Rules
Printed and bound in Great Britain by
Mackays of Chatham plc

www.simonsays.co.uk

Contents

CHAPTER ONE

An Unwelcome Visit

Ben Arnold sighed and sat back against the wall of the tree-house, brushing a strand of straw-blond hair out of his eyes. The book he had been holding slipped to the floor, where peachy mid-morning light sliding through gaps in the planks illuminated a picture of a huge dinosaur confronting a band of ancient hunters dressed in animal skins. The tyrannosaurus, its alarming mouth agape to reveal an array of massive, sharp teeth, looked down upon the tiny ant-men out of one vast, intelligent eye. It looked slightly puzzled, Ben thought, as if it was wondering why these strange little creatures were making such a noisy fuss. Or even why they were there at all – waving their pathetic-looking spears even though all the dinosaur was doing was meandering along trying to find a little breakfast – since, according to Mr Malarkey at school, dinosaurs and human beings had never even walked the Earth at the same time in history.

Then another thought struck Ben: what if the author of the book had known that all along? What if the story was not actually set in this world at all, but in another place entirely: a place where miracles and monsters, dinosaurs and dragons, goblins and ghouls, selkies and sabre-toothed tigers, all coexisted? A place he had once visited.

He looked up. Above him, spirals of dust motes filtered down from the roof of the treehouse turning gold as they passed through the rays of sun. Just like little streams of magic. It made him think of his mother; and that made him feel sad.

'Morning, Sonny Jim!'

The head of a small black-and-brown cat with shiny amber eyes appeared suddenly through the opening to the treehouse.

'The name's not Sonny Jim,' said Ben. 'It's Ben.'

This exchange had become something of a running joke between the two of them. He grinned, despite his gloomy mood.

The little cat – known by many as the Wanderer, and by Ben as Ignatius Sorvo Coromandel, or Iggy for short – regarded him with his head cocked on one side. After a while he said, 'She has to go back, you know.'

'I know. It's just . . .' Ben scratched his head. 'It's just – well, I'm scared for her.'

2

'Of course you are. She's your mother. But she's also Queen Isadora of Eidolon. The Secret Country is where she belongs.'

The Secret Country. The Shadow World. Eidolon. As Iggy had once described it to him, it was a place which no true human being had ever seen; a world which existed everywhere and nowhere; which lay between here and there; between yesterday, today and tomorrow; between the light and the dark; tangled between the deepest roots of ancient trees, and yet also soaring among the stars.

That had been before he had seen for himself the magic which was Eidolon, and discovered that he was a son of that mysterious place, as much as he was of the world he was in now. They called him a prince there, but he'd never been called *that* here. Lots of other names in the playground, but never *prince*.

He moved to make room for Iggy to sit beside him, and the sunlight fell across his face and shone into his eyes – one of which was a sensible hazel-brown, the other a vivid and startling green.

'I know that, too,' he told the cat. 'And I knew she had to go back soon, before she got any sicker. I just wasn't expecting it to be today.'

'She sent me to fetch you. I think she wants to talk to you.'

For a moment, Ben felt a tiny stab of envy that his mother was also able to converse with the little cat. He had thought this ability his own private gift; but it seemed that anyone touched by the Secret Country could communicate with its creatures.

Then his expression brightened as another thought struck him. 'Perhaps she wants to take me with her. To Eidolon.'

Ignatius Sorvo Coromandel looked at him sardonically. 'In your dreams.'

'Darling, don't you think you should take a warm coat?'

Mrs Arnold laughed. 'Don't fuss, Clive.' She pulled herself to her feet, steadying herself against the bedside chair, and gave her husband a big hug. 'Eidolon will provide for me.'

'Yes, you keep saying that,' Mr Arnold said, almost crossly, 'but what does it mean, "Eidolon will provide"?'

'Exactly what it says. My country and my folk will look after me, I know it.'

'Well, I'm packing your winter coat, anyway.' Mr Arnold stepped around Ben and Iggy and went thumping down the stairs.

Mrs Arnold sighed, for a moment looking tired and wan; then she saw her son standing in the doorway with the little cat sitting smartly at his feet. She smiled. 'Thank you, Iggy.'

Ben hung back uncertainly. 'Can't I come with you?'

Mrs Arnold took her son by the shoulders and looked at him steadily. Her eyes seemed greener today than they had for months, he thought; and her pale cheeks were washed with pink. She was excited about going back to the Secret Country, Ben realised suddenly: she actually *wanted* to leave them for her original home. A lump rose in his throat and he swallowed furiously, unable to say anything.

'Iggy will carry messages for us, won't you, dear?' She

reached a hand down, and Ignatius Sorvo Coromandel bobbed up on his hind legs to rub his cheek against it, purring like a motor.

'It would be my honour,' he growled in his strange gravelly tones, which sounded just like the voice of an American detective who lived on whisky and cigarettes.

'Besides,' Mrs Arnold added, 'you've already been very brave, Ben, rescuing my folk and getting them back to Eidolon; but I don't want you taking any more risks.'

The evil petshop owner Mr Dodds (who in the other world stood eight feet tall, had the head of a dog and was known as the Dodman), in league with Mrs Arnold's brother, Awful Uncle Aleister (known in the Shadow World as Old Creepie), had been stealing magical creatures out of Eidolon and selling them. Dragons, to be used as garden incinerators; mermaids and selkies, to adorn rich people's lakes; sprites, to be used as fancy lamps; sabre-toothed tigers and direwolves, to be hunted for sport; unicorns and satyrs, pterodactyls and dinosaurs, to be enjoyed by private collectors. But away from their home in Eidolon the creatures had sickened and died. And each death reduced the sum of magic in the Shadow World, and made Mrs Arnold sicker and sicker.

And that was not the worst of it.

Uncle Aleister was in prison now, and the Dodman had fled: no one knew where he was. But he had left an unsettling message for them.

Tied to the gate by a knotted string had been a big black bird with orange eyes: a mynah bird that he had last seen in the petshop. 'You have not heard the last of the Dodman,' it had declared. 'He will come for the Queen. And when he does, nothing in the world will stop him; indeed, nothing in *either* world.'

Ben had been so horrified by this threat that he had kept it to himself, and with each passing day it had become more difficult to speak about. But now his mother was about to walk right into the Dodman's hands . . . He hung his head.

Seeing his downcast face, Mrs Arnold felt her heart pierced. She caught him to her. 'Look after your sister and your father for me, won't you, Ben?' she said with her nose buried in his hair.

He stepped back sharply. 'You said *sister*, not *sisters* – does that mean you're taking Ellie with you, then?' he asked jealously.

Mrs Arnold smiled sadly. 'No, love,' she said, 'I'm taking Alice.'

Ben looked at her in horror. It was bad enough when she had been going back on her own: but how would a tiny little baby survive the dangers of the Shadow World?

'You're *what?*' Mr Arnold had appeared in the doorway with his wife's soft blue wool coat folded over his arm. 'Did I hear you right? You're thinking of taking the baby with you?'

'I *am* taking Alice with me, yes, dear.'

Mr Arnold sat down suddenly on the bed as if his knees had given way. 'I admit that I don't understand all of this,' he said quietly and with considerable restraint, 'but I really don't think that's a very good idea. How will you feed her? What will she do for nappies? Where will she sleep?'

Mrs Arnold patted his arm. 'Eidolon will provide,' she said. 'Alice belongs in Eidolon. She will be its next Queen.'

'What?' Ben's older sister, Ellie, stood in the doorway with her hands on her hips. Her cheeks were flushed and the make-up was smudged around her eyes as if she had been crying.

'Oh, Ellie.'

'Why's *she* going to be Queen? Why not me?'

'Now, now, Ellie,' said Mr Arnold, 'that's not really the point—'

'I want to go to Eidolon. Ben's been!'

Mrs Arnold put her arms around Ellie, and Ellie promptly burst into tears.

Ben looked at his father. They both rolled their eyes. Ellie could be a drama queen, but Queen of Eidolon? Ben thought not.

Iggy jumped up on to the bed. 'Now, now, Eleanor,' he growled. 'Queen Isadora must go back to her country: it will not be forever, and when the balance between the worlds is restored, you can visit her there. But it would be too dangerous for you now, for you have less of its magic in you than do Ben or Baby Alice; and your father would not survive there long at all, being a Dull and entirely human.'

Mr Arnold heard all of this merely as one long and rather raucous miaow, but Ellie narrowed her eyes at her brother. 'I want—' she began, pouting; but at that moment the doorbell rang.

Mr and Mrs Arnold exchanged worried glances, then Mr Arnold crossed quickly to the bedroom window. Outside, parked askew, partly on the pavement and partly across the next door neighbour's driveway, blocking the gate, was a large black Range Rover with shiny new wheels and shiny new paintwork.

'Oh no,' he breathed. 'It's Sybil and the awful Cynthia.'

CHAPTER TWO

Awful Aunt Sybil and Awful Cousin Cynthia

'Just thought we'd drop by for a cup of tea,' Sybil announced, walking straight past Mr Arnold and heading into the lounge. There, she eyed the brimming suitcase on the floor with interest. 'Going somewhere nice, are you?' she called back over her shoulder.

Aunt Sybil had always been extraordinarily nosy, but her daughter was far worse. Awful Cousin Cynthia pushed her way into the sitting room and shoved her big raffia handbag at her mother, who peered into it unsurely, then clutched it to her large chest and watched as her daughter threw herself down by the suitcase and started poking through its contents.

First of all, Cynthia pulled out a pair of supple leather walking boots and a thin green cloak. These she discarded boredly, strewing them on to the floor along with a pile of baby clothes which she'd also excavated. Other uninteresting items followed. But a moment later she came upon a battered old book. Her hand hovered over its ancient leather cover, then she picked it up and flicked through it with a puzzled expression on her face. No words appeared to have been printed on its pages, yet Cynthia's eyes scanned the open spread as if she was reading. When Ben came into the room, she closed it hurriedly and threw it down on the heap of clothes.

'Hey!' said Ben. 'You shouldn't be—'

His next words were snatched away by sheer astonishment, for at the bottom of the case something gleamed invitingly.

'Oh!' Awful Cousin Cynthia exclaimed. Dislodging a toothbrush, a bar of soap, a towel and a bottle of Calpol in the process, she grabbed something out and examined it in delight.

It was a crown. Not a heavy gold crown, studded with big flashy jewels and lined with velvet and fur, like the ones Ben had been taken to see in the Tower of London; but a delicate, spiky cap all of silver and crystal and a strange polished stone gleaming in different shades of gold and green.

With a sudden flurry of speed no one had seen from the invalid in many months, Mrs Arnold spun through the door to the lounge, pushed past the rotund shape of Awful Aunt Sybil and snatched the crown from Cynthia's hands before she could plonk it on her head.

'I believe that's mine,' she said firmly, extracting it from Awful Cousin Cynthia's talon-like grip and burying it swiftly back in the recesses of the suitcase before Aunt Sybil could see what it was – though she craned her neck so hard it looked as if it might snap.

'Not for long,' Cynthia muttered, fixing Mrs Arnold with her malicious little eyes. 'Not for long.'

Mrs Arnold held Cynthia's gaze steadily. Then she said something so softly that no one else in the room could quite catch it, and Cynthia looked away suddenly, her cheeks blazing. Mustering as much dignity as she could manage in a mini-skirt and a pair of clumpy platform wedges which did nothing for her scrawny white legs, she retrieved her horrible handbag and minced out into the hall.

'Don't bother about a cup of tea, Mum,' she said to Aunt Sybil, 'they'll only try to poison us.'

'Oh,' said Aunt Sybil, looking very flustered indeed, 'but I wanted to . . . ah . . .' She stopped, her chins wobbling. Then she caught Mr Arnold's arm and leant in close to him. Even Ben, standing several feet away, could smell the waft of her awful perfume. 'Clive, ah . . . you see, with Aleister . . . um . . . away for a time . . .'

'Three years, I believe?'

'Ah, yes . . . well, um, well I . . . that is, we, Cynthia and myself are . . . well . . . I'm coming up a little short on the bills this month and well . . . I wondered . . .'

Mr Arnold's smile came slowly, and then widened and widened till it almost spread from ear to ear. He had endured Aleister and Sybil's taunts about his low-paying job at the local newspaper and his family's humble lifestyle for a very long time; and it had been more than a touch satisfying to help put an end to the trade in Eidolon's exotic creatures, which had been the source of this much-flaunted and ill-gotten wealth.

'Sybil, dear, I'd love to help . . .' He spread his hands helplessly. 'Perhaps if you sold the Range Rover, got something a bit cheaper to run. It is an awful gas-guzzler, and well, you don't really need an off-roader around Bixbury . . .'

Aunt Sybil's chest swelled alarmingly.

Ben intervened. 'I'm sorry,' he said, catching his aunt by the elbow and steering her out into the hall, 'but we're already running late. Perhaps some other time?'

If Aunt Sybil was surprised by this sudden authority from her usually tongue-tied nephew, she didn't say so. Indeed, although her mouth kept opening and closing like a goldfish's, she left the house without uttering another word. Ben watched her get into the Range Rover and slam the door – rather more loudly than was necessary merely to close it.

Outside on the gatepost, Ignatius Sorvo Coromandel stood with his back arched and the fur of his tail sticking out like a toilet-brush, staring into the vehicle with loathing. He let out the most terrifying hiss, then a string of swear-words which made Ben gasp.

'Wow! I didn't know cats *knew* words like that!'

12

Iggy swivelled a fiery glance at his friend, then transferred his attention back to the car.

As the Range Rover pulled away, Ben spied a familiar face peering out of a raffia handbag propped against the rear window. The face was small, triangular and hairless. Wrinkles of skin pooled around its nose and slanted yellow eyes as it hissed back at the Wanderer.

Ben shivered, despite the sun on his back. 'Oh no,' he muttered. 'It's the Sphynx.'

Mrs Arnold sat slumped on the sofa, rubbing the tops of her arms. Goosebumps had popped up all along her pale skin. She was trembling. Mr Arnold sat down beside her. 'Are you sure you're feeling strong enough to . . . er, travel?' he asked carefully.

She nodded. 'I must. The time has come.' She gripped his hand. 'I'm sorry, Clive. I should have told you everything right at the start. But you'd probably have thought I was mad.'

Her husband smiled lopsidedly, as if it was an effort. 'But you *are* mad, my darling: that's why I love you. I always knew you were different from all the other women I'd met. But at least now I know why.'

'Keep an eye on Cynthia, won't you? And I don't want Ellie or Ben going round to King Henry Close.'

'I don't think there's much danger of that,' her husband said grimly.

'No way!' said Ben, coming in with a now normal-looking Iggy in his arms. 'I'd rather go to the *dentist* than round to Cousin Cynthia's!'

That made Mrs Arnold laugh. 'It *is* about time you had another check-up.'

'Oh, Mum . . .'

She smiled. 'Maybe when I come back,' she said softly. Which made him feel a little better about everything.

CHAPTER THREE

Aldstane Park

The Arnolds' rusty old Morris crawled through the streets of Bixbury, carefully avoiding the roads around King Henry Close. Mr Arnold drove; Mrs Arnold sat beside him with her winter coat folded in her lap; while in the back, Ellie and Ben sat all squashed up beside Alice's safety seat. Ignatius Sorvo Coromandel had stretched himself along the parcel shelf and was watching the baby with curious amber eyes.

'Alice,' he rasped, 'can you hear me?'

In response, the baby laughed and babbled and banged her toy – a soft pink piglet in a dress and ballet shoes – against the front of her seat. In the sunlight her eyes were greener than ever,

15

Ben thought: as green as limes, or frogs, or that green goo in tubs that he and his friend Adam had mock-fights with.

'What did she say?' he asked the cat quietly.

'Well,' said Iggy, considering, 'I think it went sort of like this: *la, la, gaga caa* . . .'

'Oh,' said Ben. He thought about this for a moment. 'And what does that mean?'

'Search me,' said Iggy.

'Stupid,' said Ellie scornfully. 'She's only a year old: of course she can't speak yet.' She gave the baby a sharp look. 'Queen-in-waiting or not.'

At the top of the road, Mr Arnold pulled into the car park and they all got out. Ben helped his father wrestle the suitcase out of the boot while Ellie and his mother released Baby Alice from the straps of her seat.

Alice waved her arms around in delight. '*Ca . . . ca . . . cat!* she suddenly said, quite distinctly. And in case anyone was unsure of what she meant, she pointed straight at Iggy, who was stretching out his back legs against the sunwarmed tarmac.

Iggy stopped his exercises and stared at her. 'What did you say?'

Alice folded the pig-doll to her chest. 'Cat,' she replied, entirely matter-of-factly, and gazed back at him out of the depths of her wide green eyes. 'Cat.'

'Oh my,' said Mr Arnold. He rubbed his hand across his face, then looked at his wife. 'Did she really say "cat" or am I going mad?'

'She did,' Isadora said fondly.

'It's a bit . . . well . . . precocious at one, isn't it?'

Ignatius Sorvo Coromandel.

Ben heard this as a sort of tickle at the back of his skull, as if a small spider had got in there and was running around. He looked sharply around, but no one else appeared to have heard it. He frowned.

'She's a very special little girl,' said Isadora Arnold brightly. She looked down at the baby and smiled. 'That was a very good first word, Alice. I'm sure by the time we come back you'll have lots of other good words to show off to your daddy.'

Mr Arnold looked unhappy. 'None of them are likely to be "Dad", though, are they?'

Ben watched as Ignatius Sorvo Coromandel – the Wanderer – took on the task of expedition leader and began a weaving trail across the park. Mr Arnold followed, supporting his wife – who was still not very strong – with an arm around her waist. Ellie carried Baby Alice, and Ben lagged at the back. Partly this was because he was lugging the suitcase, which was pretty heavy, and partly it was because cold dread seemed to dog his footsteps, almost pulling him backwards.

Aldstane Park did not look much like a place which would inspire dread; indeed, it looked very different to the last time Ben had seen it. Then, it had been pitch-dark, except for the swirling blue lights of the police cars come to arrest Uncle Aleister. But now it was swathed in sunshine and covered with people. There were families picnicking on the grass, men with their shirts off and girls with their skirts hitched up over their knees to make the most of the sun, couples entwined around one another on colourful blankets, people throwing frisbees, dogs chasing balls, and children splashing in the boating lake – where once upon a time Ben had seen a girl turn into a seal.

It looks so *safe*, he thought, and all the people look so happy. They certainly don't look as if they know there's a standing stone amongst the rhododendrons which is the doorway to another world. A world full of wonders and weirdness. A world full of dangers . . .

And he felt the shadow of the Secret Country fall across him, chill and dark. But when he looked up, it was only a cloud which had passed across the sun . . .

For a famous explorer, Iggy often proved to be remarkably inefficient at finding his way; and now was no exception. First, he took them on a winding route between the bushes that brought them out by an ice-cream van and a queue of noisy children; next, he circled around on himself till they finished up exactly where they had come in.

'Oh dear,' he said, looking as embarrassed as only a cat can look. 'I could have sworn the Aldstane was around here somewhere.' And he started to groom a paw furiously in order to divert their attention from his error.

Ben sighed. 'Follow me.'

With the suitcase bumping against his leg, he led his family back into the cool darkness between the rhododendrons.

And at last there it was: a great finger of rock partially hidden among a grove of hawthorns. Pitted with age and patched with lichen, it was sunk deep in the earth, deep in the leaf mould. You sensed that, like an iceberg, there was more of it below the ground than appeared above.

A weary smile touched Mrs Arnold's face. 'Ah,' she breathed. 'The waystone.'

She turned to her husband. 'Do you remember when you first came upon me, Clive?'

'How could I ever forget?' Even as he spoke, Clive Arnold could picture the scene in his head: a delicate pale-skinned girl dancing with her eyes closed and her silver-blonde hair lit by shafts of sunlight in a clearing in this very park, fifteen summers before.

'This was the stone by which I entered your world,' she said softly.

'Cool!' said Ben. He grinned, despite his anxieties. 'It's where I went into the other world, and where Iggy came in, too.'

Mrs Arnold reached a hand down and stroked the fur on top of Iggy's head. The cat, who up to this point had still been looking slightly miffed that Ben had been the one to find the Old Stone rather than him, purred.

'Look,' said Ben, pointing.

Partly obscured by growths of lichen, a pattern was visible on the surface of the rock. It consisted of a lot of straight lines and angles and was topped by an arrow, pointing down into the ground.

Mrs Arnold ran her hands across the stone.

'E-I-D-O-L-O-N,' she spelt out.

'Eye-do-lon,' said Alice. She gurgled delightedly. 'Eidolon.'

Ellie almost dropped the baby in shock.

'Whoo!' said Ben. His little sister had never seemed odd to him before – well, no odder than any other baby – but now he felt the hairs rising on the back of his neck. 'Whoo, that's weird!'

'Clever girl,' whispered Mrs Arnold. 'Such a clever girl.'

Mr Arnold had gone white. 'Izzy,' he said at last, 'don't go. You've been better these last couple of weeks. Perhaps you'll just keep getting better if you stay here—'

He would have said more, but at that moment there was a shimmer of rainbow light around the base of the Aldstane, and something emerged from the stone.

CHAPTER FOUR

The Centaur

The first thing any of them saw was a leg, but it was not the leg of anything human. Sleek and brown, it ended in a shining hoof. A second leg followed almost immediately.

'What the—?' started Mr Arnold.

A body was now beginning to appear: the smooth brown chest of a man which melded seamlessly into the powerful torso of a horse. A moment later, the entire figure stood before them.

'Darius!' cried Ben.

'It's a cent . . . a centimetre . . . a sentiment . . . a . . . er . . . centipede . . .' Ellie stuttered.

21

'Actually, he's a centaur,' Ben supplied scathingly. 'His name's Darius and he's a Horse Lord.'

Ellie stared, her eyes getting rounder and rounder. She loved ponies and had just started to find boys very interesting indeed: but this amazing apparition appeared to combine the best of both worlds. The top half of the centaur was that of a young man, with a proud, fine-boned face and piercing eyes. Black hair fell to his shoulders and tanned, well-muscled chest; but from the waist down he had the body of a horse.

'Hello,' she said, blushing even more.

Darius clenched a fist to his chest and gave her his fierce smile. 'Good day,' he said. 'Princess.'

Ellie giggled and looked sideways at her mother. Then she put a hand to her mouth and gazed up at the centaur through her fringe, in what she thought was her most alluring pose; but to her disappointment the Horse Lord was not looking at her any more.

'My lady, forgive me, I did not see you there . . .'

With fluid grace, Darius dropped to his knees before his Queen, his head bowed and his fists crossed, but Isadora Arnold took two steps forward and touched him on the shoulder.

'Please get up, Darius,' she said softly. 'I have been away from my country for too long to expect such an honour.'

Mr Arnold looked from the centaur to his wife in some kind of shock. He had always loved and been amazed by Isadora; but he had never before seen her so regal or imposing. Even Ben and Ellie exchanged glances. To them, she was

'Mum' – a bit daffy; always talking to inanimate objects, as well as to flies and dogs and caterpillars; a mother who looked after them and laughed with them and was more likely to get tired than to get angry. It was hard to think of her as a queen, especially of a magical realm.

Darius got to his feet and stood there uncertainly. Then he said, 'Cernunnos sent me through the wild road to fetch you—'

'Cernunnos is the Lord of the Wildwood,' Ben interrupted knowledgeably. 'He's big and sort of greenish, and he wears leaves, and stag's horns.'

'Leaves?' Ellie sounded scornful. 'Who'd want to wear leaves?'

But already in her head she was fashioning herself a fetchingly skimpy outfit of autumn colours designed to show off her dark hair and hazel eyes to their best advantage, the sort of dress which would beguile a young Horse Lord.

'He sounds a bit, well – wild,' Mr Arnold said nervously to his wife. 'I mean, stag's horns . . .!'

'Cernunnos is my loyal friend,' Isadora Arnold replied gently. 'He guards the deep forest and takes care of my people there. He will take care of me and Alice, too.'

'But – but, you can't live in a forest!' Mr Arnold said in horror. 'I mean, where will you sleep?'

'The mossbeds of Darkmere are famed throughout Eidolon,' his wife said teasingly. 'You should try them sometime; but –' as she saw him open his mouth to say something '– but not now, Clive, dear; the Shadow World is not a safe place for those without magic at the best of times – and now is *not* the best of times.' And she passed Baby Alice into Darius's outstretched arms.

The centaur cradled the child, smiling as she reached up to wrap her fingers in his long black hair.

Alice looked out at the assembled group as if she was already Queen and they were all her courtiers. 'Da . . . Da . . .'

Clive Arnold held his breath.

'Da . . . Da . . .'

'Go on, love, say "Dad" . . .'

'Dar . . . ius!' Alice declared triumphantly.

And everyone laughed. Apart from Mr Arnold. First of all he looked crestfallen; then he fixed the Horse Lord with a stern glare. 'Just how did this Cernunnos know my wife was coming here today?' he asked, suddenly suspicious.

The young centaur returned Mr Arnold's gaze steadfastly. 'The Lord of the Wildwood did not know exactly when our lady would return, only that it must be soon,' said Darius. 'Since she has been away my people have waited for her to come back to us, and many have sickened and died, or been stolen away. Without our Queen, we are diminished. But when Ben came to us, we regained hope; and every day since he returned to your world I have kept vigil by the entrance to the wild road and waited and listened until I felt the signature of her magic drawing near. There will be great rejoicing in Eidolon that its Queen has returned. Now we have a chance to unite our folk against the Dodman and drive him from the Shadow World forever.'

Mr Arnold looked puzzled. 'The Dodman?' He turned to his wife. 'Who is this Dodman?'

Isadora Arnold looked discomfited. 'Maybe it was not entirely wise to mention that particular problem at this moment,' she said to the centaur, who put a hand to his mouth, too late to draw the words back.

'He's awful,' Ben said. 'Over here, he was just Mr Dodds who ran the Pet Emporium; but over there, he's about eight foot tall and has a great big dog's head! And he has some rather nasty goblins as his helpers, and some savage hounds—'

'That's quite enough, Ben,' his mother said firmly. She put her arms around him and whispered in his ear, 'I know all about the Dodman, and his mynah bird, and the message it carried. That's why I must go back now and face him.' She stepped away and regarded her son with her head on one side. Then she dropped him a slow, conspiratorial wink.

'I don't like the sound of any of this at all,' Clive Arnold said. 'If you're determined to go, I feel I must come with you.'

'Oh, Clive, I know you would if I asked you. But who's going to look after Ben and Ellie if you come to the Shadow World with me?'

Mr Arnold hesitated. 'I suppose Sybil—'

'No way!' chorused Ben and Ellie in one horrified breath.

Their father looked at them unhappily. 'No, I don't suppose that would work.' His shoulders sagged in defeat. Then he turned to address the centaur. 'You'd better look after my wife and daughter,' he said fiercely.

Darius bowed his head. 'I would give my life for them,' he said simply.

Clive Arnold nodded brusquely and blinked his eyes very fast as if he had something painful in them.

Ellie gave her mother a short, fierce hug, and wouldn't look at her.

'Take care of your dad for me, won't you, darling?' Mrs Arnold asked her; but Ellie didn't respond, just stood there looking at her shoes. They were big, cork-soled sandals with bright flowery patterns all over them, but even so Ben couldn't imagine why she found them so fascinating.

Now Mrs Arnold came to her husband. 'It won't be forever, Clive,' she said softly, and kissed him quickly before he could say anything.

Ellie looked up and rolled her eyes. But when she caught the centaur watching her, she blushed so hard that even her ears went red.

'Come along, Ignatius,' the Queen of Eidolon said. 'Time to go.'

'What?' Ben couldn't believe his ears. He looked at Iggy, his heart sinking fast. It was bad enough that his mother and little sister were going away: but the black-and-brown cat had become his best friend. 'Are you going too?'

Iggy shifted uncomfortably. 'Um,' he said. 'Well . . .'

'If he's going to carry messages for me, he needs to know where I am,' Mrs Arnold said gently. 'Or he'll never find me.'

That was all very well, Ben thought, but knowing the cat's hopeless sense of direction, how would he find his way back?

He'd probably end up in Alaska or Antarctica or Outer Mongolia. But he didn't say anything. He couldn't: there was a huge lump in his throat.

He watched as his father helped his mother on to the centaur's back, and once she was up there, held his hand against her cheek. Then Mr Arnold took Alice from the Horse Lord and passed the baby up to her mother. Ben gave the suitcase to Darius, who stared at it uncertainly, then fitted a hand around its handle and hauled it up into his arms, cradling it as he had the baby.

Mr Arnold tucked the blue woollen coat tenderly around his wife, and Alice waved her pig-doll at him.

'Da . . .' she said. 'Dad. Daddy.'

Mr Arnold gave her a wobbly smile.

Then Darius turned and plunged into the standing stone. First his head and forelegs vanished, followed by the suitcase, the Horse Lord's long neck, Mrs Arnold with Alice held tightly in her arms, and finally the centaur's powerful hindquarters and long black tail.

Ignatius Sorvo Coromandel jumped into Ben's arms and butted his forehead against his friend's cheek. 'See ya later, Sonny Jim!'

Amber eyes blazed into Ben's and then the little cat, too, was gone, into the Secret Country.

Ellie and Mr Arnold stared at the Aldstane in disbelief. Ellie walked all around the stone, testing the ground with her clunky sandals. Suddenly she exclaimed, 'Oh!'

Her foot was nowhere to be seen.

'Ellie . . .' said her father warningly.

She pulled her foot back and it reappeared, detail by detail.

'Come along,' Mr Arnold said quietly. 'Let's go home.' He looked absolutely exhausted.

'I'll come in a minute. I need a few moments to myself,' Ellie declared with the tragic demeanour of a Victorian heroine.

Ben and his father exchanged glances; then Mr Arnold shrugged. When Ellie got in one of her moods there was little point in arguing with her. 'We'll wait for you by the car, then,' he suggested. 'Don't be long.'

They made their way out of the rhododendrons and into the brightness of the park, where the sudden ordinariness of their surroundings – the Labradors and lovers and children with ice lollies dripping down their tops – seemed even more surreal after all that had just taken place. Ben and Clive Arnold walked in silence for a while until Ben, sensing the waves of sorrow emanating from his father, could bear it no longer. 'Do you remember the dragons, Dad?' he asked in an attempt to cheer him up.

Mr Arnold smiled, for a moment looking almost happy. He stared up into the brilliant sky. 'It's hard to believe I've been up there on the back of a dragon named Ishtar.' He paused, thinking. 'She was an ancient Babylonian goddess, you know.'

'Wow,' said Ben, awed. 'I didn't think she looked *that* old.'

His father grinned, despite himself. 'Not the dragon, silly: the Ishtar in *our* world's mythology. They called her the Lady of Battles.'

The Ishtar Ben knew was Zark's wife. Ben had rescued the

dragon Zark from the clutches of Awful Uncle Aleister, who'd
been planning to sell him for dogfood, since Zark hadn't been
a great success as a garden incinerator, which was what Uncle
Aleister had sold him as. He had, however, been a terrific success as a Range Rover incinerator. Ben remembered with some
delight how its paint had bubbled and its tyres had melted
down into horrid black goo. Thinking about the dragons made
Ben's heart lift. There were wonders in the world after all: in
both worlds. Then he thought: perhaps all the dragons will
unite to help Mum win her kingdom back. He imagined flights
of them, like Second World War fighter squadrons, storming
through the skies of Eidolon . . .

Spreading his arms like a Spitfire, he went zooming and
zigzagging through the picnickers all the way back to the car
park.

Sitting in the old Morris, Ben and his father waited for Ellie.
And waited. And waited. They often had to wait for Ellie – for
her to wash her hair or 'do' her face, or change her clothes eight
times even though they were only going to the supermarket –
but she couldn't have any of those excuses now. At last Mr
Arnold sighed and looked at his watch. 'I'd better go back and
look for her.'

'It's all right,' said Ben. 'I'll go.' It made sense: he knew
exactly where the stone was.

His father tousled his hair then sat back in the car seat
glumly, while Ben belted away through the gates.

Ben scanned Aldstane Park, looking for his sister's bright

pink T-shirt amongst the crowds. But Ellie wasn't by the ornamental fountain. She wasn't at the boating lake. She wasn't sitting on the grass, nor on any of the benches beside the path. She wasn't in the queue at the ice-cream van. She wasn't hiding in the shadows between the rhododendrons; and she wasn't at the Aldstane, either.

Ben's heart began to thump, though that might have been because he was out of breath from all the running.

'Ellie!' he shouted, when he got his wind back. 'Ellie, where are you?'

But the only sound that returned to him was the faint echo of his voice.

And there, at the base of the stone, was a flowered sandal.

Suddenly Ben knew, with a painful thump of his heart, that Ellie had gone through the Aldstane into the wild road beyond. She was in the Shadow World.

CHAPTER FIVE

In the Court of the Dog-Headed Man

The Dodman sat back in the carved wooden throne in the great hall of Dodman Castle and stretched out his long, long legs. He had renamed the castle the previous day from its boring original name of Corbenic Castle, and was still very pleased by the new version. He wondered why he hadn't thought of it before . . . Old Creepie would have moaned on about it: that was why; he liked to stand by tradition, and the castle had been called Corbenic Castle since anyone could remember. Aleister Creepie was the Queen's brother. The castle had been his home, too, when the pair of them had grown up here. But now Aleister had a rather different residence: a prison cell in the Other World, for the next three years. But the Dodman was not entirely unhappy about this, even though Old Creepie had been his ally. The situation had its advantages. Another of the royal family of Eidolon was out of his way. Now he had only to get rid of the Queen and her annoying family, and the Secret Country and everything in it would be his.

Not that he would stop there . . .

The Dodman looked around at his motley courtiers. Lolling on the benches over the remains of a vast feast, sat a number of squabbling goblins, two terrifically ugly trolls and a cross-eyed giantess arrayed in a bizarre costume of leather and spikes. A pair of what appeared to be chicken's feet protruded grotesquely from her gaping mouth. They were still kicking.

The Dodman looked at the huge bones left over from this, which lay scattered like a desecrated graveyard all over the long table and the floor beneath, and gave them all a disgusted look, which went unnoticed. He had plans for this place: for his kingdom. Bit by bit, he would drain the magic out of the Secret Country so that none could challenge his rule. He had made a good start on this plan, keeping as much magic for himself as he dared, draining it out of the small folk he captured, drinking it down. One day, he promised himself, this hall would be crowded with the great and the bad of Eidolon – gorgeous, glittering and greedy for the power only he could give them. That day must surely come soon. 'Peasants!' he snorted, looking around him again and shaking his head.

'*Squarrrk!*'

The mynah bird which had been sitting on the crest of the throne behind him lifted suddenly into the air. 'Peasants!' it echoed, taking roost up in the rafters.

The Dodman kicked the goblin lying on the floor in front of him, snoring drunkenly amongst the dogs, and, when it didn't stir, put his feet up on it – which was the only thing it was useful for.

The dogs were the Gabriel Hounds, his spectral hunting pack. They were not well behaved. No one had ever been able to teach these ghost-dogs any manners, and the addition of the Horned One's wolves had not helped matters. Today was not any different. A furore started up between the hounds and the wolves, and his unfortunate footstool was peed on once and bitten twice during the fracas before he could pull them apart.

There was a cough from the back of the hall, and the Dodman looked up. A visitor had appeared, materialising as silent as a ghost in the great hall's doorway.

It was the Sphynx.

'So, what news? Was the Queen preparing for a journey?' The Dodman's eyes – as round and black and shiny as a pair of giant ball-bearings – narrowed minutely. 'To Eidolon?'

'Yesss, master. I saw the thingsss she packed with my own eyesss. She had the Book with her and—'

'The Book, you say?' The dog-headed man grinned fiercely. 'The Book of Naming?'

'Yesss, lord. There was no mistaking it. And,' the speaker's voice lowered, 'she isss bringing the Crown of Eidolon back with her!'

'That worthless trinket!' the Dodman growled dismissively. 'I need no crown to be King of the Shadow World!'

In fact, he wanted the crown very much: but he knew it wouldn't fit him, not with his gigantic dog's head.

'Of course not –' the visitor paused '– sssire.'

The Dodman's dog-mouth widened into a sharp-toothed smile. 'Yes,' he said, 'I like the sound of that. *Sire.*' He sprang to his feet and at once the hounds and wolves were everywhere, snapping and snarling and picking fights with each other.

The creature started and ran pell-mell between the dogs and under the throne, where it sat quivering, its long thin ratlike tail sticking out into the light. After a moment it seemed to realise this and turned around quickly, before anyone could bite its bottom. Its wedge-shaped pink face and slanting yellow eyes peered out at the dogs.

'Don't let them get me, ssssire . . .' it begged piteously.

In response, the Dodman reached down and swept the Sphynx up by the loose skin around its neck, allowing it to dangle precariously over the snapping jaws.

'Now then, little spy,' he said, tightening his grip so that the creature writhed, torn between fear of the hounds and terror of the Dodman. 'Who is coming with her? Is it the odd-eyed princeling? Or maybe your friend, the one with the skinny legs and bad hair?'

The spy drew its feet up convulsively as one of the Gabriel Hounds got a bit too close for comfort. 'My fr-friend?' it gasped.

The dog-headed man gave the visitor his ghastly grin, the firelight gleaming on his fangs. 'Your little friend, Cynthia.'

'Cynthia? N-no. She would never travel with Isssadora. She hates the Q-queen.'

'Are you sure?'

'Q-quite sure,' the spy replied nervously. As it felt the Dodman's grip relax slightly, it twisted out of his grasp, turned in mid-air, dug all four paws into his arm and, righting itself, fled up along his shoulder and leapt on to the top of the throne, where it sat, shivering and glaring out at the scene below it with loathing in its eyes.

The Dodman rubbed his arm where the cat's sharp little claws had dug into him. 'You had better be right about this,' he told it. 'You say the Queen is coming soon?'

From its new position of relative safety, the Sphynx smiled enigmatically. 'Oh, yesss,' it declared. 'She hasss already set out. She may already be in Eidolon for all I know.'

And before the dog-headed man could recapture it and ask it more difficult questions, it gathered its haunches and sprang over the pack of hunting hounds, ran across the great hall and out of the door.

The Dodman watched it go. He knew it would be back, for it craved the treats he gave it in return for the information it brought him – the gnomes' eyes and fairy-wings, the phoenix livers and fillet of mermaid-tail, all manner of delicious items it could come by nowhere else in either world.

'Grizelda!' he yelled, and the giantess lumbered to her gigantic feet. 'Leash the hounds and bring them to me. We are going to capture ourselves a queen!'

CHAPTER SIX

In the Shadow World

One minute, Eleanor Arnold had been looking at the old standing stone in Aldstane Park, and the next, some mad impulse had overtaken her and she had stepped *into* it, and been swallowed up by it in a way she could not comprehend. Whirling around and around as if on some weird fairground ride, she had felt sick with dizziness and thought she might faint. Air had rushed past her, warm with the scents of an English park; then turning chill and finally freezing, until at last the wild road ejected her with such force that she tumbled head over heels before coming to an abrupt halt. Now, she sat on the ground, rubbing her knees and shins and staring about her with absolutely no idea where in the world she was. Her skin prickled all over as if someone had sprinkled itching powder inside her clothes. She looked about, scratching absent-mindedly. Then she sneezed – six times.

'Wow,' she said. 'I must be allergic to something.'

At school everyone had at least one allergy that they boasted about; but Ellie had never really had a proper one before.

On the other side of the stone it had been a hot and cloudless summer day; but here – wherever 'here' was – it was decidedly wintry. An icy wind blew through the trees, rattling the dying leaves and whistling through the branches. Frost etched the bare soil: the ground was as hard as iron.

Ellie jumped up, and almost fell down. Something was wrong with her balance! In the fall through the wild road it seemed that one of her legs had unaccountably grown longer than the other. Or had one got shorter? She stared at her feet. One of her sandals was missing. That was annoying! They were new, and no one else had a pair like them. They were her favourites. She stared around in search of the missing shoe. But she couldn't see it anywhere. In fact, she couldn't see anything very well. It was as if the fall had done something funny to her eyesight, so that for the first time in her life she needed glasses. She rubbed her eyes and blinked and looked around again, but still the world was slightly blurry and out of focus.

Never one to admit to being in the wrong, Ellie now suddenly regretted her rash decision to step through the stone. But for once there was no one but herself to blame. Indeed, there seemed to be no one else around at all.

'Mum?' she called. Her voice sounded for a moment like the plaintive cry of a seagull, and then it was whisked away to nothing by the wind. She called again, louder this time. 'Mum!' And then, more hesitantly: 'Darius?'

But no one answered.

Ellie, who was wearing only a short-sleeved pink T-shirt and a pair of thin cotton jeans, began to rub her upper arms vigorously. Perhaps it would be a better idea to go back. But there was no sign of the Aldstane at all. Hot tears pricked at the back of Ellie's eyes but she blinked them away fiercely. It would not do for anyone in this strange place to find her crying: besides, crying made her eyes go all red and puffy, and everyone knew that was not a good look, especially if you wanted to make a favourable impression on a handsome young centaur.

'Well,' said Ellie aloud. She often spoke to herself: it was a trait she had inherited from her mother, who spoke to all sorts of things, including herself, all the time. 'I'll start walking in one direction and see what I can see.'

She looked around, finding that if she squinted, the world seemed to come into sharper focus. She was standing in a small clearing between trees: but no matter in which direction she turned, trees and more trees were all she could see. No houses, no streets, and worst of all, no shops.

'Hmmm,' she said, feeling dismayed. Given a choice of preferred environments, she would select first of all clothes stores, then make-up counters, shoe shops and internet cafés. Gardens came pretty low down her list of favourite places to be; forests lower still. 'It would be quite easy to get lost here.'

Then she remembered something Ben had told her about a story in one of his books of mythology. She couldn't quite recall the point of the story, only something about a handsome youth and a king's daughter and a kiss and a labyrinth. It was the kiss she remembered most clearly; the rest of the story was a bit of a haze, but she thought the king's daughter might have given the boy a ball of red twine so that he could mark his route through the maze and not get lost. If she were to do something similar, she could at least find her way back to where she was now . . .

But Ellie didn't have a ball of red twine, or indeed anything that might substitute for it. In her little handbag all she had was: some make-up, a mirror, a pen, some chewing gum and her mobile phone. This, she seized upon with sudden excitement. She turned the phone on, punched in a number and waited. And waited. And waited.

After a long time the screen blinked. Then it offered a message:

No network coverage

Ellie glared at it. Obviously the signal was a bit weak here. She walked on a little way and held the phone up, but the left side of the screen indicated no change to the signal strength. Annoyed, she tapped out a swift text and pressed 'send'.

For a long time she peered at the tiny blue phone, which seemed to be working very hard. Then at last something flashed on the screen:

Message not sent
Try again later

Ellie said a word her father would have told her off for using and threw the phone back into her bag. Perhaps if she were to head for higher ground she'd be able to get a signal.

She squinted about her. Trees. Trees. Trees. Some covered in moss, others in ivy. The ground looked pretty flat; but if she walked far enough surely there would be a hill. She started out in one direction, hobbling on her one remaining sandal (to lose both would be really stupid), then turned back. She really ought to mark her way somehow . . .

She looked around desperately. Ivy! She could lay a trail of ivy which she could follow back here if the route she chose turned out to be a false start. She grabbed a handful of ivy on the nearest tree and started to pull it away from the trunk.

'Ow!'

Ellie jumped backwards as if something had bitten her. She looked around, but there was no one in sight. Frowning, she approached the tree again and checked behind it. Not a soul. Eventually she shrugged, decided she'd been hearing things, and gave the ivy another tug.

'Ow! Stop yanking my hair, you little witch!'

As if out of nowhere a face materialised in front of her. Ellie shrieked and fell over in shock. When she looked up again, a figure was leaning out of the tree. Ivy flowed over her shoulders just like hair, her skin was as smooth and sheeny brown as the casing of a conker, and she wore a dress of bark

41

and moss. Her hands were balled into fists. Her eyes sparked green fire.

'Oh, you're not the little witch. You smelt a bit like her, though.'

Ellie frowned. Clearly the thing, whatever it was, was quite mad.

'How dare you attack me for no reason!' the tree-creature went on. 'There's been too much of that sort of thing, and worse. But there will be justice soon, now that the Queen has come back to us, just you wait and see.' And she shook her finger at Ellie angrily.

'The Queen?' Ellie's heart leapt up. 'Have you seen her? Which way did she go?'

'Why would I tell you such a thing?'

'Because she's my mother!' Ellie picked herself up and rubbed all the manky old leaves and soil off her best jeans with some annoyance.

The creature watched her with narrow eyes. Then she stepped out of the oak and made a progress around Ellie, examining her from top to toe. 'You don't look much like a princess . . .'

Ellie tossed her long dark hair and was horrified to find a spider hanging off it. She brushed it away in disgust. 'Who are you to say that?' she said crossly. 'You're just some tree-thing, all covered in scabby old bark and ivy—'

'—and your eyes are the wrong colour to be the true child of Queen Isadora. Besides, I am not a "tree-thing": I am a nymph.'

Ellie had no idea what a nymph was, and cared even less. 'I can't help the colour of my eyes!' she snapped back. 'My dad's got brown eyes. But he comes from . . . Earth.'

The tree-nymph burst out laughing. 'Is he a worm, that he comes out of the earth?'

'How rude you are! First you call me a witch, and then you call my dad a worm.'

'And you call yourself a daughter to our Queen!'

'I *am* her daughter – her eldest daughter. Then there's Ben – he's a boy, and Alice – who's just a baby—'

'Ben . . . and a baby . . . ah, now you're beginning to make some sense.' The nymph leant forward and scrutinised Ellie closely. One of her twiglike hands reached out and caught the girl by the chin, turning her head this way and that. The tree-nymph's fingers were cool and smooth against Ellie's skin, and the searching eyes were the rich green of new leaves, but Ellie wrenched her head away, and sneezed and sneezed and sneezed.

'Bless you,' said the nymph. 'There *is* something about you . . . But how did you get separated from the Queen, if she really is your mother?'

'She came through the wild road with . . . Darius, the Horse Lord,' Ellie said quickly, feeling a blush coming on. 'I followed a little later.'

'I know the Horse Lord, Darius. And I know of the boy, Ben. Maybe you are telling the truth after all,' the tree-nymph said at last. 'It has been hard to trust anyone in Eidolon for a long time.' She paused, considering, then appeared to come to a decision. 'The Queen passed through this way, heading east, towards the domain of the Horned Man, Cernunnos. If you follow the sun as it goes down, you cannot go far wrong.'

Ellie looked up into the wintry sky. It was cold and white, and if there was any sun at all, it was hidden behind thick clouds. She shivered. 'I can't see the sun,' she said miserably. 'Which way is east?'

But the tree-nymph was not listening to her. She was staring above Ellie's head and her eyes were wide with consternation. In the distance behind her Ellie could just hear a faint wailing sound, like the cries of many lost souls tossed about in the wind, and even though she did not know what it could be, it made the hairs rise on the back of her neck.

She turned to follow the tree-nymph's horrified gaze, but all she could make out was a fast-moving blur.

'Run!' cried the nymph. 'Run, run for your life!'

But Ellie was still squinting for a better view. The moving shape came on and on, until at last she could just about make it out. Up in the sky, silhouetted against the white clouds, there appeared to be a great chariot bearing a number of bizarre figures, including one that looked just like a gigantic dog in a suit. The chariot was drawn by a pack of creatures which seemed to flicker in and out of visibility.

'Wow,' said Ellie, initially impressed. Then she remembered what Ignatius Sorvo Coromandel and Ben had told her about Mr Dodds, who in this other world stood eight feet tall and bore the head of a great black dog. A cold feeling spread through the pit of her stomach. 'Oh, no . . .'

In panic, she whirled around to follow the nymph to

whatever place of safety she might have found for herself – and discovered that she had vanished.

'Thanks a lot!' Ellie hissed into the empty air. She had never much liked trees and now they were pretty close to the top of her hate-list. Awful Cousin Cynthia was first, still; closely followed by her awful mother, Aunt Sybil.

She hobbled back the way she had come, her handbag thumping against her hip, but the design-spec for her pink-and-silver-flowered wedge-heeled sandals hadn't made escaping from monsters in aerial chariots a top priority. Even when wearing both she could only manage a fast mince. In one, it was hopeless. Within seconds, Ellie was sprawled in a heap amidst the tree roots and leaf mould, howling in pain and rubbing a turned ankle. The remaining sandal lay, broken-strapped, a little distance away. The Dodman was pointing triumphantly down at her, and the Gabriel Hounds were circling in on a space in the forest canopy and preparing to make a landing . . .

CHAPTER SEVEN

The Wildwood

Many leagues west of where Eleanor Katherine Arnold was nursing her sprained ankle, Mrs Arnold – known in Eidolon, the world of her birth, as Queen Isadora – thought she detected the passage of something sinister overhead and stared up into the dense web of branches, her keen eyes searching for the source of this unnerving sensation.

'Don't look up,' Darius urged her softly, his neat hooves picking a silent way through the frozen leaves. 'It's the Gabriel Hounds. Remember: if they feel your eyes upon them they will become aware of you and be drawn back this way. We are close to Cernunnos's domain now: only a few more minutes and you will be safe in the Wildwood.'

Isadora shuddered, and not just from the freezing wind. In the Other World there was a phrase for feeling so suddenly uncomfortable and scared: there, it was said to be like someone walking over your grave; but in Eidolon they said, 'I can feel the breath of the Gabriel Hounds on my neck.' Now that saying was far too close to the truth.

'Are they looking for us?' she breathed. She glanced down at Alice, but the baby was fast asleep, clutching the pig-ballerina like a last vestige of her old life.

Darius turned to look at her over his shoulder. 'I fear so, my lady. Though how the Dodman could have known you'd entered the Shadow World I do not know. I took secret paths to and from the waystone and only the tree folk noted our presence.' He paused. 'Things have come to a terrible pass indeed if any of them would betray us to the Dodman.'

'I am sure my nymphs and dryads would never fail us so,' Mrs Arnold said softly. But she could not help but frown.

They moved in silence into the shadow of the deep forest. Here, the air was warmer, and from beneath the eaves of the ancient trees many eyes watched their passage.

Then the whispers began:

'*Look, it's her. It is.*'

'*She doesn't look much like a queen.*'

'*Look again: see her eyes.*'

'*Ah, green, so green.*'

'*It is the Queen.*'

'*It is, it is: it's Isadora.*'

'*Isadora, she's come back to us.*'

'*Isadora.*'

'*Queen Isadora.*'

Gnomes and goblins, sprites and dryads – one by one they slipped out of their hiding places, where long habit and a sense of self-preservation had driven them during all these years, and gazed in awe upon the Queen of Eidolon as she returned to this sheltered corner of her realm from a world of which they had no knowledge. One by one they came out, and one by one Isadora acknowledged them with a glance. To other eyes, they might have seemed strange or ugly creatures indeed: some had the rough, brown, lumpy skin of toads; some had ears that grew pointed and fleshy out of their heads like great mushrooms. Some of the fairies were ancient and toothless, their wings lacking lustre; some had lost their wings altogether and bore only long, skeletal fingers where the gauzy film had been eaten away by age or disease. Still others were pale and attenuated, as if they had grown up out of the light; and a few were bright and shiny and looked brand-new. But to Isadora each of them was brave and beautiful.

They walked farther into the cool depths of the forest and it was now with a grain of fear in her heart, that Mrs Arnold noticed over and over how there was mildew on the leaves of the bushes they passed, poisonous fungi and strangling vines leeching the life out of the trees on which they grew. No birds sang. Even the famed mosses of Darkmere were no longer the brilliant emerald they once had been.

Fifteen years! She had been away for fifteen years, and the health of Eidolon was failing just as her own health had while she was away from it. All those creatures stolen and dead, all their magic lost. A world abandoned to wickedness and greed, to her silly, weak brother and the dog-headed man who had exploited his ambitions so ruthlessly. She hoped she could set things right again: to have left Eidolon for love now seemed a selfish choice. But if she had not met Clive, then Ellie, with her moods and teenage tantrums, Ben, with his silly jokes and his kind heart, and tiny Alice, whose personality was yet to be determined, would not exist in either world.

> *One plus one is two*
> *And those two shall make three*
> *Three children from two worlds*
> *Will keep Eidolon free*

She remembered embroidering these words on a small square of white linen when she was little more than a child herself: then, it had seemed just a nonsense rhyme. Now she wondered whether there could indeed be such a thing as prophecy. *Three children from two worlds*. Ben and Ellie had already had a part to play in beginning the rescue of Eidolon; and Alice would one day be Queen after her: so perhaps it was true after all.

She sighed, missing Ellie and Ben already.

At last, the path carried them past a stream. On its pebbled shores lay the silvery bodies of fish. Iggy sniffed at them and recoiled in disgust.

Isadora frowned.

'My goodness,' she said. 'If a greedy cat won't eat a fish there must be something badly wrong.'

'Greedy? Me?' Iggy stared at her reproachfully.

Darius turned his head. 'We do not know why they are dying,' he said, 'except that they are already rotten by the time they die and any who have been so hungry as to try to eat them have ailed. Cernunnos fears the waters have been poisoned; even Ia the undine, that tough old biddy, has been under the weather, and the naiads have no more energy than to lie around in the shallows. No longer do we hear their laughter in the Crystal Pools, and the songs of the mermaids are gone from the Dark Mere.'

Mrs Arnold firmed her jaw. 'These things must be remedied. The Dodman shall steal and poison and terrorise my folk no more.'

She looked fierce and determined, but tears glittered in her eyes. Darius looked away sharply. It was too much to see his Queen weep: it spoke of hopelessness, of despair.

At that moment a cry ripped through the still air – a great hullabaloo of triumph and bloodlust.

Iggy's fur stood on end from his ears to the tip of his tail. He knew that awful sound too well. 'The Wild Hunt . . .'

Darius wheeled about, shading his eyes. 'They must have happened upon some poor wayfarer.'

Mrs Arnold's hand tightened in the centaur's mane. 'We must go to their aid!'

Behind them, the Wildwood seemed to sigh, and when

they turned back, a great dark figure had appeared between the trees. The Queen stared grimly ahead; but when the figure moved out into the light her features relaxed.

'Cernunnos!'

The stag-headed man halted before her and dropped swiftly to one knee, so that the great branches of his antlers obscured his face.

'My lady, my Queen.'

Slipping from the centaur's back, Isadora took two steps towards him and touched his shoulder.

'Lord of the Wildwood, rise. In this forest realm we are equals: I would not have you kneel to me.'

Eyes the colour of a moorland tarn, brown as peat, gold as honey, found hers and he rose solemnly. 'You must stay here, my lady, with Darius: here you are safe. Unlike the unfortunate quarry the Dodman and his hounds have run to ground. I will discover who the poor soul is and whether they can be rescued.'

And with that he was away, his feet as fleet and silent as a deer's, slipping swiftly into the shadows until he disappeared from sight.

Darius watched the Horned Man go, an unhappy expression on his handsome face, and Isadora could tell that whatever duty he felt to her and Alice, he badly wanted to follow the Lord of the Wildwood. Instead, he put the suitcase down by the side of the stream and began to pace back and forth in an agitated manner, as if he could not bear to be still.

Mrs Arnold watched him. Then she turned to the little cat,

who was now sitting on the suitcase, his tail flicking up and down.

'Run after Cernunnos, Iggy,' she said softly, 'and bring us news as fast as you can. I am sure that something is terribly wrong. I feel it here . . .' She touched a hand to her heart.

Iggy shivered. His last encounter with the Dodman and his hounds had not been a pleasant one. He had a sudden, unbidden and entirely illogical thought: what if it was Ben who was in danger? Galvanised by this, he jumped down from the suitcase, took to his heels and bolted into the undergrowth.

The Horned Man's track should have been easy to follow for a cat of Ignatius Sorvo Coromandel's parentage, for both his mother and father were famous explorers, and such aptitudes often run in families. His mother, Finna Sorvo Farwalker, had founded a colony in the New West and discovered the wild road into the Valley of the Kings; while his father had climbed Cloudbeard, the highest mountain in Eidolon. But somewhere along the line Iggy had failed to inherit their skills; and before long he was hopelessly lost in the middle of a vast thicket of brambles.

Never one to admit defeat, Iggy ploughed on, but the thicket became denser and denser and soon he was forced to crawl on his belly. Snagging fingers caught in his tail and coat as if dragging him back. Something sharp embedded itself in the side of his neck.

'Bother!'

There were now so many bits of bramble and thorn stuck in

his fur that it would take an age to groom them all out. He felt like a pincushion. There is very little in the world a cat likes less than to be uncomfortable; except, perhaps, to be hungry. It took a few stern words to remind himself that there was someone else – possibly Ben – out there experiencing a good deal more discomfort than he was, and he steeled himself to carry on.

'I wouldn't go that way if I were you!'

Iggy looked up, then to his left and his right, until at last he found the speaker.

A little red-and-white striped snake with a frilled collar of skin was watching him from a safe distance, its forked tongue flicking in and out of its mouth.

Iggy did not like snakes. He did not like the way they slithered, nor the way they coiled themselves around your leg if you trod on them by mistake, nor the way they tasted when you bit them, not by mistake. Chicken, indeed! Everyone knew that only chicken tasted like chicken: snakes tasted of snake.

Besides, a red-and-white striped snake, especially one with that ludicrous frill, was probably poisonous. Putting his head down, he rummaged further into the thicket.

'I said, I wouldn't go that way if I were you!' the snake repeated, this time with an edge of annoyance to its voice.

'Well, you're not me,' Iggy muttered.

Luckily, snakes tend to have very poor hearing, and this one was no exception, for it said no more and, giving what might have been in a creature with shoulders a sort of shrug, wove its way between some roots and disappeared.

'Good riddance!' Iggy declared firmly.

He shoved aside a particularly fierce blackberry runner, dislodged a large thorn from his head, and pushed onward until eventually he thought he could see daylight ahead.

That's a relief, he thought to himself. I was beginning to think I was in trouble there.

But just as he was congratulating himself on getting himself out of a sticky situation, a truly horrible smell permeated the thicket. A sort of rancid, rotten smell that got into your mouth and nose and coated your fur with something vile and greasy.

Head down, teeth gritted, eyes watering from the stench, Iggy crawled the last few feet through the brambles into the pale winter sunlight and sat there breathing as shallowly as he could manage. Then he looked around him.

All about lay bones. Piles of bones; heaps of bones. Bones scattered as if someone had been playing a game with them. Bones discarded as if after a jolly good gnawing. Fishbones, sparrow bones, sprite bones, and the bones of things which looked as if they might once have belonged to something rather bigger – rats, maybe; rabbits or (and now he gulped) cats . . .

The next thing he knew, a huge shadow had blocked out the weak light of the winter sun, the smell had enveloped him like a cloud, and he was swinging up into the air by the scruff of his neck.

'Got you!' declared a guttural voice.

Iggy twisted his head to look at his captor – and immediately wished that he hadn't.

CHAPTER EIGHT

Prisoner

By the time Ben got back to the car park his father was looking very worried indeed; and when he saw that Ben was on his own, he went pale.

Ben had been vainly hoping that maybe, just maybe he had missed his sister amongst the crowds and that he would somehow find her back by the car, even though he knew deep down that he would not. 'She's gone,' he reported quietly. 'She's gone into the wild road. Into Eidolon. She left this behind.' And he held up the flowered sandal.

Mr Arnold stared at it. All the colour went out of his face.

Then he let his head drop against the steering wheel and banged it there repeatedly. 'Stupid, stupid, stupid girl!'

When he sat up again there was a red mark with a Morris symbol imprinted on his forehead.

He lurched out of the car. 'Well, I suppose we'll just have to go in and bring her back again.'

Ben looked dubious. 'Mum said it would be bad for you. Eidolon, I mean.' He watched his father's eyes narrow. 'It's just that you . . . well – you don't have . . .' He ground to a halt, not sure how to say it without hurting his dad's feelings.

'I don't have what?'

'You don't have any magic in you,' Ben finished in a small voice.

Mr Arnold snorted. 'There's no such thing as magic, son,' he declared. 'Only tricks.'

This from a man who had flown on the back of a dragon.

Ben shook his head. 'There's magic in Eidolon, and everything that belongs to Eidolon. I've got some in me, and so have Ellie and Alice, because of Mum – but you haven't. And that's why the creatures of the Secret Country get ill when they're here: there's no magic in this world. So I suppose that's what Mum means – it'll be like that for you there. If you go into a world that is full of magic, you'll get ill, just like they do when they come here.'

Mr Arnold thought about this for perhaps three seconds. Then he roared, 'Nonsense!'

He stomped around to the back of the car, opened up the boot and pulled out an anorak, an umbrella, a pair of wellies, a torch and a small rucksack. He put on the anorak and the

boots – despite the boiling heat – stuck the torch in the rucksack and turned to Ben, flourishing the umbrella. 'Right!' he
said. 'Ready for anything.' He dug in the other pocket and
pulled out a packet of paracetamol. 'You see – if I feel ill, I can
take a couple of these. Bound to be fine!' He beamed at his son,
and Ben had the sudden sinking feeling that his dad was actually looking forward to having a bit of an adventure.

Reluctantly, Ben followed in Mr Arnold's long stride,
almost having to run to keep up with him. Was it so surprising
that Ellie wouldn't do as she was told, when their father didn't
listen to anyone either?

On the edge of the rhododendrons, Mr Arnold had to give
up the lead to his son, and Ben wove through the hawthorns
and hollies to where the Old Stone stood, ancient and brooding
in its shady place. His father, refusing to be in awe of it,
marched over to the stone and started prodding it all over as if
looking for a hidden lever or door handle.

'Here,' said Ben.

At the back of the Aldstane he pushed one foot gingerly
into the secret highway, and watched his father's face change as
his shoe vanished from sight. For a moment, Ben thought he
might have changed his mind, but: 'We'd better hold hands,'
Mr Arnold said firmly. 'I don't want to lose you, too.'

Together they stepped into the wild road.

Ellie wasn't fond of dogs at the best of times, and now was definitely not the best of times. Once, when she had delivered
papers for some extra pocket money (a job which had lasted

exactly one day), she'd had a bit of a run-in with the yappy poodle at Number Four, which had sunk its nasty yellow teeth into her new fake-fur coat and hung on for dear life, growling and drooling, until its yappy owner had come out and proclaimed that poor little Maurice had obviously mistaken Ellie for a bear come to maraud Lower Bixbury, and was only doing his job as a guard-dog. Ellie had marched back to the paper shop, quit on the spot and never worn the coat again.

But the dogs which faced her now were certainly not poodles. Despite the fact that they were sort of transparent, they looked as if they could do a lot more damage than Maurice. Luckily, they appeared to be harnessed to the big chariot which had just landed, for although they stretched their ghostly necks out at her and snapped and snarled and foamed at the mouth, they didn't seem to be able to reach her. Ellie drew a big sigh of relief.

But behind the ghost-dogs, there came leaping over the side of the chariot a host of creatures with dark-green leathery skin and pointed ears. Before she could get to her feet, the goblins were confronting her, chattering and grinning and showing off their horrid pointed teeth.

'She doesn't look much like a queen!' one cackled.

'Too fresh and tasty . . .'

'Like a little nymph . . .'

'Or a mermaidy . . .'

'Without a tail . . .'

They looked down.

'No tail,' they agreed.

One of them came forward and poked at Ellie's bare arm with a sharp black fingernail. 'Mmmm,' it declared. 'Nice soft skin.'

For a second all Ellie could think was: *well, at least the papaya and parsnip body lotion works.* Then: '*Wew!*' she wrinkled her nose and drew back against the tree, so disgusted that she almost forgot to feel afraid. 'You stink!' Then she started sneezing and couldn't stop.

The leading goblin cocked its head at her and grinned. It sniffed its armpit, gave a considering nod and then offered this noisome part of its anatomy to its nearest companion for inspection.

The second goblin inhaled deeply and nodded. 'Terrible,' it agreed. 'Really terrible.'

Soon they were all smelling one another and giggling appreciatively.

'Vile!'

'Horrid!'

'Like rotten eggs!'

'No, like dead rats!'

'Bat poo!'

'Trolls' feet!'

'Dinosaur farts!'

'Minotaur wee!'

They looked at each other. 'Nah,' said the leading goblin, looking wistful, 'not as good as that.'

'I wish.'

'He's the king of bad smells.'

While the goblins debated this fascinating point, Ellie tried to get up. The ground was cold against her bare foot, but the offending sandal lay several metres away. As she put her weight on it, a searing pain shot up through the ankle she had twisted.

'Not so fast, my dear.'

Suddenly a great black shadow had blocked out the light and there was a heavy weight on her shoulder, pressing her back down on to the freezing ground. Ellie looked up, and wished she hadn't.

The figure which loomed over her stood over eight foot tall, and wore a sharply-cut black suit topped by the long-snouted head of a jackal.

'You'll have a lot more to worry about than bad smells where you're going!' the Dodman growled menacingly.

'Yes!' giggled one of the goblins. 'We're going to mash you up with rats and lizards and worms and dead fairies, and put you in a pie!'

'You can't put me in a pie!' she cried in sudden outrage. 'I'm a princess!'

Now all the goblins started to wheeze with laughter.

'A Princess Pie!'

'Yum!'

'With spider sauce!'

'BE QUIET!' the Dodman roared. He glared around at the pack of them. 'Or I'll rip you apart and feed your giblets to the dogs.'

That shut them up.

He leant in to take a closer look at Ellie. Rage flickered in his shiny black pupils like inward fires, and Ellie closed her eyes in terror as his hot breath beat against her face, certain he was going to bite her head clean off. Then she sneezed, right in his face.

The dog-headed man recoiled in disgust, wiping his muzzle. 'Princess, eh?' he growled.

Ellie cursed herself silently for her stupidity. Then, gathering all the courage she could muster, she opened her eyes and looked him squarely in the face. 'That's just something my friends call me,' she said. 'It doesn't really mean anything.' Using the tree for support, she pushed herself to her feet, and looked at her watch so that she didn't have to look at the dog-headed man any more. Curiously, the readout said '16.25.03', which was the time when she had entered the waystone in Aldstane Park. It felt much later than that here, for the sky was darkening; yet the seconds were no longer ticking by, as if time itself was frozen, or no longer relevant in this other world. Not wanting to think about the implications of this, Ellie added brightly, 'Goodness, is that the time? I must go, or Mum and Dad will be worried.'

The Dodman grabbed her wrist. His cold, sharp dog-nails dug into her skin. She shuddered.

'We don't have watches in Eidolon,' he said, and his black eyes scanned her face avidly. 'So where have you come from, I wonder, and how have you got here?'

Ellie felt her legs tremble. She remembered what the goblin had said about her not looking like the Queen. They must have come here looking for her mother. Tears began to well up inside her. She decided to let them fall. Crying often got her what she wanted, and what she wanted now was to escape from this horrible world.

'I . . . oh,' she sobbed. 'I got lost in Bixbury Park while . . . hiding from my friends and . . . sort of fell against this big . . . stone . . . and then next thing I knew –' she turned bleary eyes up to the dog-headed man '– I was here in this awful place. Oh . . . I'm lost – can you help me get home?'

For a moment it looked as if the Dodman's heart – if he had one – might be softened by her distress, for he hesitated as if considering her request. Then something stirred in the branches above her head and a familiar voice hissed, 'Oh, I don't think that would be advisable at all, ssssire. The young lady you hold prisoner is indeed the Princesssss Eleanor.'

Everyone looked up.

Ellie squinted hard. There was a small pale shape up in the tree, the shape of a pinkish creature with big pointed ears.

It was Cynthia's cat.

CHAPTER NINE

A Fish out of Water

'Oh no!'

Ben stared helplessly up into the dark Eidolon sky, in time to see the spectral glow of the Dodman's carriage drawn by the ghost-dogs speed past overhead like a nightmare version of Santa Claus's sleigh and reindeer.

'What?' said Mr Arnold, rubbing his eyes. He stared upwards short-sightedly, rubbed his eyes again. 'What is it?'

'It was the Dodman,' said Ben grimly, staring after the disappearing apparition. 'And the Wild Hunt. They must be out looking for Mum.' He paused. *Or Ellie*, he thought to himself.

'Ellie!' Mr Arnold bellowed so loudly that Ben almost jumped out of his skin. 'Eleanor! Where are you? Get back here at once!'

'Ssssh!' Ben looked around apprehensively. He grabbed his father's arm. 'Someone might hear.'

Tutting, Mr Arnold clicked the torch on and shone it around the clearing. The light bounced from tree to tree, illuminating a strand of ivy here, a fallen log there; a patch of gnarled bark, the twiggy fingers of a leafless alder, a tangle of bramble runners.

'Darn thing!' Mr Arnold declared. 'Batteries must be as dead as dodos.' He shook the torch violently, and its golden beam shot erratically around the clearing and up into the branches of a huge old oak, alarming whatever small resident was hiding there. Something long, thin and pale scurried out of sight.

'But it's working fine,' Ben said, mystified. He took the torch from his father's hand, swung the beam from one side of the clearing to the other and gazed around. The trees stood out starkly against the empty night air, sharply delineated by the harsh yellow light. 'See?' he said, holding the torch steady so that it lit a circle of dying ferns.

'I can't see a thing,' Mr Arnold said crossly, taking back the torch.

Ben stood in its beam. 'Can you see me?' he asked.

The light played across his features, illuminating his one green eye and one brown eye, the pupils gone to pinpricks in the glare.

Mr Arnold frowned. 'Not very well,' he admitted. Suddenly he looked anxious. He rubbed his eyes again, held his hand up in front of his face. 'It's very strange,' he said softly, 'but I don't seem to be able to see anything much here.'

'Ah,' said Ben. He closed the eye he thought of as his Eidolon eye, and at once the world became a bit blurry and distorted. Then he closed his Earth eye and looked around with his Eidolon eye wide open. Everything leapt into sharp focus.

He had forgotten about that.

'It's the Secret Country,' he said. 'It's different to home. You shouldn't be here, Dad, you're not adapted for it.'

Mr Arnold braced his shoulders. 'Nonsense,' he said. 'It's just very dark and the torch isn't working properly. You lead on, son. I'll be fine.'

Ben sighed. If he were to admit it to himself, he didn't have a clue where to begin looking for Ellie. He had hoped she would be on the other side of the waystone, lost and a bit anxious, ready to return home after making a silly mistake; but his sister could be remarkably pig-headed when she chose to be. He picked a careful path among the trees with his father's hand on his shoulder, and walked for several minutes amusing himself with the image of Eleanor's skinny body topped by a pig's head. A definite improvement, he decided at first. Plus, she'd have rather less use for her massive collection of make-up; although as soon as he thought this, the original image was replaced by an even more nightmarish one – of Ellie's new pig's face adorned with false eyelashes, shimmering green eyeshadow and a lipsticked snout. *Gross!*

He was so carried away by these horrific details that he forgot to look where he was going – and the next thing he knew he had stumbled over something on the ground and his father had cannoned into him, knocking him flat. The torch shot out of his hand and rolled away down the slope.

'Ouch!' said Ben. Something hard was digging awkwardly into his kidneys. He sat up and extricated the object.

It was the other one of Ellie's ridiculous shoes, and the ankle-strap was broken right through. Ben felt his heart beat faster. There was no way his sister would be parted from both of her beloved sandals unless in very exceptional circumstances. They were her favourites, though Ben thought they were horrible, with their chunky soles and lurid, swirling flowers. And they made her walk like a clumsy camel.

Retrieving the torch, he swung its beam around the area. The ground was rather churned up, as if by many feet, and further back, where there was a space between the trees, two deep ruts had parted the frozen ground amongst the dead leaves, ruts which could have been made by huge wheels. Like the wheels on a chariot, Ben thought desperately, remembering the ghost-dogs' carriage . . .

'Dad,' he started, but when he turned back it was to find his father sitting on the ground, clutching his head and groaning.

'It's nothing,' he said, when Ben came over to him. 'Just a bit of a headache. I'll be fine in a minute, once I've taken some tablets.' He dug in his pocket and brought out the packet of paracetamol he had brought from the car.

'Dad,' he began again. 'I think Ellie's been captured.'

But Mr Arnold did not seem to be paying attention: he was trying to dry-swallow one of the pills; but without any water to wash it down with it stuck obstinately to his tongue, making him cough and retch.

'Dad—'

'Yes, yes,' Mr Arnold said impatiently, in between coughs. 'I really must get rid of this headache. It seems to be getting worse all the time.' He pushed himself to his feet and stood there, swaying unsteadily. 'Goodness, I do feel rather odd.' Abruptly, he sat down again.

Ben grabbed his father's arm and tried to haul him upright. 'Listen to me,' he said loudly, 'I think the Dodman has got Ellie. We have to find her.'

Mr Arnold turned a wan face up to Ben. 'I don't think I'm going to be much use to anyone unless I can get these pills down,' he said after a while. 'Do you think you could find a stream or something and get me a drink of water?'

Ben closed his eyes. It was all too much: his father was ill, his mother and baby sister and his friend Iggy had gone with the Horse Lord to who knew where, and his elder sister appeared to have been taken by the Dodman, and here he was in the dark, in another country. Suddenly, the Shadow World felt like the alien, wild and terrifying place he had always known it to be in his heart of hearts.

It would have been easy to give up then, to admit defeat and slump down on the ground to await whatever fate might bring them. The human-boy in Ben considered this option for perhaps three seconds, before the Prince of Eidolon took over.

'Dad, you have to get up and walk, whether you think you can or not,' he said with sudden force. 'These woods may once have been Mum's domain, but she's been away for a long time and all sorts of dangers lurk here now. We can't just sit here and wait for them to find us, and someone has to save Ellie. If you're not well enough to help me do that, I'll get you to the waystone and you can go back through the wild road into Aldstane Park.'

It was probably the longest speech Ben had ever made to his father – worse even than explaining why he'd been given detention for misbehaving in class with some paper pellets and an elastic band, that had made a brilliant catapult but had unfortunately overshot his target – a horrible boy called Ian, whom he had once caught tying a firework to a cat's tail – and hit Mr Mapp, the geography teacher, instead.

For a moment Mr Arnold forgot how ill he was feeling, so overcome with surprise was he at the vehemence of his usually mild-mannered and slightly shy son. His mouth dropped open, but no words came out. Then, slowly and painfully he shambled to his feet. 'It was my choice to come,' he muttered obstinately, 'and I'll have to make the best of it. Besides,' he grinned weakly, 'can't let the rest of my family have all the adventures while I sit at home, can I?'

Ben led his father through the trees until at last they came upon a lake. Ben sniffed at the water cautiously. 'Only a sip,' he warned, though it smelt okay.

Mr Arnold took his headache tablets. As they sat on the bank waiting for the pills to take effect, an almost-full moon slid out from behind her mantle of cloud and laid a silvery sheen across the water, illuminating the spiky reeds and the fronds of a willow which dipped its icy fingers in the lake. It was a tranquil place and Ben's heart started to beat at its normal speed, until something – a bat, or a very large moth – flittered overhead. For a moment he thought it might be the wood-sprite, Twig. But even with his Eidolon eye he couldn't make out what it was before it disappeared into the trees.

'It seems beautiful here,' said Mr Arnold after a moment. His breath emerged in a great cloud of vapour. Then that vanished too.

'It is.' Ben shivered. He wished he'd brought some gloves. He stuck his hands in his pockets and found there, amongst a number of assorted items, some toffees. He offered his father one and together they sucked the sticky paper off and sat there chewing silently.

'If you think this is beautiful, you should have seen it fifteen years ago.'

The voice, which sounded rather as if the speaker were talking and gargling at the same time, seemed to be coming out of the deepest part of the lake. Ben stared. There was a splash, as if something had just submerged; then bubbles rose to the surface, limned in moonlight. These were soon followed by what appeared to be a head. Alarmed, Ben shone the torch at it. It must surely be a very big fish indeed to have such a loud voice and to produce such large air bubbles.

From the middle of the black water, hands waved weakly in the sudden flood of illumination. '*Aiee!* Stop, please . . . The light, make that terrible light go away!'

Taken aback, Ben shut off the torch.

Once more in darkness, the figure regained some of its composure and stopped flapping its hands around. All Ben could see was what seemed to be a perfectly normal, human-looking head with a lot of white hair which floated limply on the surface of the lake.

'Who are you?' he asked.

The figure swam closer. 'The question is, who are *you* to have the power to wield a sunbeam in the dark of night?'

Ben laughed. 'It's not a sunbeam,' he said. 'It's a torch. It runs on batteries and when I click this switch it comes on. Look . . .' He turned the torch on briefly and the circle of yellow light offered him the vision of a very old woman staring back at him in terror. Her eyes were droopy and red-rimmed and sore-looking, and her skin was crusted with scales.

'*Aieee!* Don't look at me!' She covered her face with her hands.

Ben turned the torch off.

'What sort of fish is it?' his father asked, peering myopically into the darkness. 'It's making a very strange noise.'

'It's not a fish, Dad,' Ben said. He shrugged. 'I don't really know what it is.'

'Fish? *Fish?!*' The voice rose to a shriek. 'Visitors to the Dark Mere never used to be so rude!'

'I'm sorry,' Ben said. 'My father cannot understand the folk of Eidolon: he is not of the Shadow World. My name is Ben. My mother—' He stopped himself in case he said too much, then added carefully, 'My mother comes from here, though.'

'Ben, did you know you were talking to yourself? One of your mother's habits,' Mr Arnold said wistfully. 'They do say it's the first sign of madness.'

'Sorry, Dad: you just can't hear what this . . . er . . . person is saying.' He was about to say more when the creature in the water spoke again.

'Shine the sunbeam on your face so that I can see you,' the old woman said.

Ben did as he was requested.

There came a sharp intake of breath from the creature in the water. 'Ah, so you must be the Odd-Eyed Boy, the one they've been talking about: the one who escaped from the Dodman by diving off the battlements of Corbenic Castle. The one who swam the lake ahead of the Gabriel Hounds and summoned the Lord of the Wildwood to his aid. The one who flew on a dragon he'd saved from certain death, put paid to some of those no-good goblins and imprisoned that miserable turncoat Old Creepie!'

Ben grinned. 'Well, it wasn't quite like that; I had rather a lot of help—' he started.

'No need for modesty, young man. Or should I call you "Your Highness"?'

'Oh no,' Ben said quickly. 'I'd much rather you didn't. But what can I call you?'

The crone slipped back into the water, made a graceful turn, and with a splash, something silver gleamed in the moonlight. It was a tail: a great big fish's tail complete with interlocking scales and a huge curving fork at the end of it, just like the ones you see in storybooks.

'A mermaid,' he breathed.

The old woman cackled, and Ben saw how there were gaps and stumps between her sharp, in-curved teeth. 'Well, I was a maid once, but that was rather a long time ago now. My name is Melusine: but you can call me Mellie – they all do. Beautiful, I was then. Long golden hair and pearly skin; eyes that could drown a man. I could sing, too: oh, how I could sing! Many's the unwitting goblin I've lured into my clutches with a song . . .' She cleared her throat and began to croak:

> '*Come see, come see my loveliness*
> *Come swim, come swim with me*
> *I'll wrap you in a golden tress*
> *And take you home with me*
> *Through the lilies we'll dive down*
> *Down to where the fishies play*
> *And there in my fair arms you'll drown*
> *And never more see the light of day . . .*'

Ben gulped. It seemed highly unlikely that anyone would fall for that sort of trick, even if Melusine *had* been a great deal prettier than she was now and didn't sound like a rusty old gate-hinge.

At this point, Mr Arnold interrupted. 'Son,' he said, and

there was a distinct note of concern in his voice. 'Did that fish just sing?'

'Er, yes, Dad. But it's not a fish: she's a mermaid called Melusine – Mellie for short.'

His father gave him a weary look. 'A talking mermaid? In a lake in another world?' He rubbed a hand across his face. 'Well, anything's possible, I suppose.'

'It is here,' Ben agreed.

'Tasty little beasts some of them were.' The old mermaid was still reminiscing wistfully. 'Nowadays –' she gave a disgusted snort '– it's more like chewing old turnips. We've all got older and grimmer since your mother went away. It used to be that nothing aged here. It was charmed, they said; a world living under its own spell.'

'Um, my mother's back now,' Ben said. 'She came back today.'

'Oh, I know about that. There was quite a commotion.'

'Commotion?'

'All the comings and goings amongst the woodland folk. Lots of scurrying and preening going on. Me, I'm too old and ugly for all of that sort of nonsense now. I don't like people looking at me any more.'

'You're not *that* ugly, Mellie,' Ben lied chivalrously.

Melusine chuckled. 'Nice of you to try to make me feel better, and just what I'd expect from a prince of the blood. Always were a charming lot, your family.' She paused. 'Apart from Old Creepie, of course.'

'I . . . ah . . . saw the Dodman and the Wild Hunt flying

overhead earlier. Do you think they were looking for my mother?'

The crone cocked her head on one side. 'I know the noise those hellhounds make when they're on someone's trail,' she said after a pause. 'They certainly caught something: but the Queen's safe in the Wildwood; and the Princess, too.'

'Ellie?'

'Ellie?' Melusine echoed.

'Eleanor,' Ben amended. 'My older sister. She's . . . ah . . . a bit taller than me, and quite thin, and she was wearing—'

The mermaid shook her head. 'No, no, it was a baby with the Queen; but there was another girl, almost full-grown, who was getting chased by the Wild Hunt, or so I heard from the oak-nymph.'

Ben's heart sank. 'He's got her, then,' he breathed. 'My other sister, Eleanor. The Dodman has got her and taken her to the castle.'

'What's all this about a castle and Ellie?' Mr Arnold seemed suddenly galvanised. 'And the Dodman – is he the one with the dog's head and all the goblins? That doesn't sound good . . .'

'It's not,' said Ben.

With dread he remembered the deep, wide, chilly lake from which the forbidding castle walls rose like great cliffs, and the courtyard scattered with bones. It was miles away, through forest and over heath and plain. He had no idea in which direction it lay, nor how they could possibly cross the lake or get in to save his sister.

Melusine clucked her tongue. 'There's been a lot of talk

about goings-on at Corbenic. Fortifications, dungeons, strange monsters massing in the grounds, and the lake. He's gathering himself quite an army, the Dodman. And he's sucking the life out of Eidolon, too. Now he wants to extend his vile rule across all of the Secret Country: that's what I've heard.' She paused. 'So do you think that he has the Princess Eleanor?'

Ben nodded grimly.

'Then that is terrible news indeed.'

CHAPTER TEN

In the Dungeons

'Can't have you leaping out of the window and taking a swim like your annoying little brother, can we?' the Dodman said, leering at Ellie. 'So we're taking no chances this time. It's the dungeons for you, my sweet Princess of Eidolon.'

'Sweet. *Squarrrk!*' echoed the mynah bird on his shoulder.

The Dodman cocked his dog-head on one side and regarded Ellie out of the depths of one of those disconcerting black eyes. The flickering green flames of the wall-candles leapt and danced, throwing bizarre shadows over everything. Green was not a colour, Ellie decided, which brought out the best in anyone.

'A pity you do not resemble your mother more closely, for she was quite the beauty.' He stared past her at the stone wall as if he could see the image of the young Isadora imprinted there. 'She was extraordinary, you know, fifteen years ago. Her hair was as golden as a dragon's hoard; her skin was as pale and soft as a mermaid's belly; her eyes—'

Behind his back, one of the goblins stifled a giggle.

The Dodman whipped around and fixed the offender with a gimlet stare, as if he might fillet him then and there, and serve his spleen up for supper.

'And her eyes were as green as a goblin's heart,' he finished sharply.

'That's not a very nice thing to say about my mother!'

The Dodman's gaze swivelled back to Ellie, knifelike. 'How old are you, *Princess*?'

'Fourteen.'

The dog-headed man clenched his jaw. 'If Isadora hadn't conceived you, she'd have come back to me. She would have loved me, you know, if she'd allowed herself to follow the true inclination of her heart. She was always intrigued by me – if a little afraid. When she fled to the Other World it was only because she wanted me to pursue her. And pursue her I did – but I was late, too late. To think of that perfect beauty, stolen by a common human . . .'

'My dad's not common!'

The Dodman sneered. 'A creature without magic? A denizen of the Other World? Each and every one as common as muck! Millions of them, all lumbering around without a clue as to the nature of the worlds, of their origins, of their pathetic purpose in life – and before you ask, that purpose is to bow down and acknowledge me as their true monarch; to crawl on their bellies and avert their eyes from me; to offer heartfelt prayers for my well-being, and that of my bride and our line of sons—'

'Your bride?'

'Bride, *squarrrrk!*'

Ellie felt her skin go cold and goosebumpy all over. Her stomach turned over as if she might be sick at any moment. She felt dizzy.

The dog-headed man barked a sharp laugh. 'Don't flatter yourself, my dear. You're much too young and scrawny for my taste and, sadly, half-breed brunettes do nothing for me at all.'

Ellie glared at him furiously. 'I am NOT scrawny! I'm a perfectly normal size ten. Not that I'd marry you anyway, Dogbreath, not if you were the last . . . the last . . . creature in either world!'

The Dodman's eyes glinted in the gloom of the corridor. Then he licked his long black lips with a long black tongue. 'So rude, and so ungrateful. You should think yourself lucky we came upon you in the Wildwood and brought you here to offer you the hospitality of our home, rather than leaving you there for the trolls and the sabre-toothed tigers to find. They'd not have been so tender with your pampered skin: see, we have prepared the finest accommodation for you . . .'

And he unlocked and pushed open a thick, ironbound door.

It looked as dark as death inside, and it smelt awful. Ellie hated the dark: though she didn't like to admit to it she was afraid of it, of the things that might spring out at her. At home she kept a little night-light burning by the side of her bed. But it didn't look as if the cell had any light in it at all. All she could make out was a semi-circle of light on the ground in front of the door which showed bare stonework, its only carpet a layer of dust, dust which had been disturbed by the passage of many feet. Not all of them human, by the look of some of the prints . . .

'Make yourself at home, girlie,' the Dodman growled. 'Because it's going to *be* your home for a long, long time.' He paused. 'Unless your dear mother does the sensible thing.'

'What do you mean?'

The dog-headed man's long-lipped smile widened until she could see every one of his gleaming ivory teeth.

'Grizelda?'

His voice resounded from the massive stonework like the voice of a dozen Dodmen, and somewhere in the gloom at the far end of the long corridor something stirred. It came closer.

For several seconds Ellie held her breath; then, when the creature stepped into the flickering light of the wall sconces, she exhaled in a great, shocked *whoosh*. Before her, limned by the weird green light of the candles, stood the ugliest thing she had ever seen in her life. She – or at least Ellie thought it was a she, for a massive bosom appeared to be trapped behind a tattered array of leather and spikes on the creature's torso – towered above even the Dodman, and her shoulders brushed the walls of the passageway on either side. Her hair, which appeared to be bright orange even in this odd candlelight, had been twisted into a hundred lumpy dreadlocks, wrapped around with bones and feathers and teeth. Her nose was more like a snout than anything. Her cheeks were like slabs of old mutton, and her smile was like a disaster in a graveyard. But despite the unfortunate features which fate had dealt the giantess, she did appear to have some vanity left in her, for her massive lips were smeared with bright-red lipstick, some of which also coated her uneven, tombstone teeth.

Ellie regarded this vision as steadily as she could, although maintaining eye contact was a bit difficult when the beast's eyes looked in two different directions at once. Then she said, forcing a friendly grin, 'You know, that shade of lipstick really doesn't do anything for you at all.' She dug in her handbag and from its depths retrieved an elegant silver tube. This she pulled apart and twisted until the cosmetic within revealed itself as a rather smart shade of chestnut-brown. 'Here,' she said, holding it out to the giantess, 'try this colour instead. I think you'll find— Oh!'

The giantess poised the lipstick tube at her mouth for a second: then the entire thing disappeared into her maw of a mouth. She chewed vigorously, the metal cylinder grating horribly against her teeth, then gave Ellie a ghastly grin.

'Tasty.'

The giantess grabbed Ellie's handbag from her, dug around in it, and pulled out the mobile phone.

'No!' Ellie wailed, but it was already too late, for the hapless phone had also disappeared down the monster's throat.

Grizelda chewed the metal, plastic and circuitry with the most blissful expression on her face.

'Yum!' she declared. She wiped the back of a huge hand across her mouth, then burped loudly. What Ellie had thought was red lipstick smeared itself grotesquely across her chin and some of it dripped on to her tunic, making a dark, shiny mark.

The Dodman rolled his eyes. 'Honestly,' he said. 'She'll eat anything. Give me the fairy, Grizelda.'

The giantess looked puzzled; or at least her expression changed to one in which her lower jaw dropped open. Something was stuck between two of her bottom teeth. It looked suspiciously like a wing, gauzy and transparent. With a swift hand the Dodman caught hold of the trapped item, flipped it out from the giantess's mouth and held it up. There was still a leg attached, tiny and delicate, shod with a long, spiky slipper of iridescent blue. Drops of red liquid oozed from it.

So the stuff all over the monster's mouth hadn't been lipstick at all, then . . . Ellie shuddered. How *horrible*; how cruel.

'Oh, for badness's sake! When I tell you to bring me things, I mean *alive*, not chewed into pieces.' The Dodman turned to the goblins and held out a huge key. 'Boggart? Bogie?'

'Yes, lord?' two of the goblins chorused. They gazed with adoration at the key.

'Go and fetch me another fairy from the storeroom. A nice big strong one. Quickly, and you shall be rewarded!'

Bogie snatched the key from their master. Boggart tried to snatch it from him. Fighting as to who got to wield the wondrous object which gave access to the most special place in the whole castle, the goblins turned and sped up the passageway, pushing and tripping over each other all the way.

The Dodman watched them go with narrow eyes. 'Clowns,' he complained bitterly. 'Things will be different soon enough. When I have a better class of minion to choose from . . .' His gaze transferred itself to Ellie. 'Well, my dear, in you go.'

He gave her a hard shove and Ellie stumbled into the dungeon. Inside, she blinked and squinted, unable to adjust to the lack of light. Behind her, the dog-headed man clicked his fingers.

'I hope you still have the sprite, Grizelda.'

The giantess mumbled something, discarded Ellie's now rather mangled handbag, then poked her huge fingers into a pouch at her side. She extracted something from it which emerged with a strange, scratchy squeal of protest. An odd pinkish light oozed past her fingers.

'Don't squeeze it so hard!' The Dodman prised the glowing thing from the giantess's huge mitt and held it up. Ellie stared at it. It was a large insecty-thing, with the iridescent wings of a gigantic dragonfly and a tiny humanlike face. Light pulsed out of it with every breath, light as red as blood. As if it could not bear to look at the awful thing that held it, it kept its eyes tightly shut.

'Twig?' Ellie gasped. Ben had told her all about his adventures in this peculiar world, about the friends who had helped him escape.

The sprite opened its eyes. They were big and dark and prismatic, many-faceted, like a ripe blackberry. It blinked at her and said something in its weird voice, something which sounded like *acorn.*

'Acorn?' Ellie echoed.

The sprite nodded. 'Not Twig,' it wheezed, and the red light flickered. 'His cousin, Acorn. They caught me in a net. In the Wildwood. Hurt me.'

The Dodman shook it viciously. 'I'll hurt you more if you don't stop your whining. Keep that light coming!'

He shone the sprite over Ellie's shoulder and illumination immediately flooded across the cell-room.

Ellie gasped. 'There's no way I'm staying in here! It's . . .' Words failed her.

The cell was small, windowless and filthy. An inch or more of dust had settled on every surface like the matted grey fur of the world's grubbiest cat – on the narrow bed, which appeared to be no more than a stone shelf set into the wall; on the uneven flagstones of the floor; on a rickety table and chair; on an old tin bucket in the far corner.

Ellie's eyes fixed upon this last detail with dread and loathing. 'What's that?'

The Dodman's smile widened. 'That, my dear,' he announced with some satisfaction, 'is your ensuite bathroom. Nothing but the best for the Princess of Eidolon.'

'For the Princess, *squarrrrk!*' The mynah bird bobbed its head and fixed her with a shiny eye.

Ellie blinked back tears of rage. 'One day my mother will punish you for this,' she declared fiercely.

'She may try,' the dog-headed man conceded, 'but by then she will be powerless against me. I shall take her magic from her, bit by bit, when she gives herself up to me.'

'And why ever should she do that? She will never give herself up to you.'

The Dodman laughed. 'Oh, I do not expect her to come willingly. I expect her to come for love.'

Ellie frowned. That sounded like a contradiction if ever there was one. 'Love? You must be mad: she will never love you.'

'Me? Ah, no, my dear. I harbour no such delusions since she fled into the arms of your father. But she loves you . . .'

The silence which settled over the scene at these words was broken seconds later by the sound of running footsteps. The goblins had returned.

'*I* caught it – let *me* give it him!'

'Nah, get off, I want the reward!'

There was a brief skirmish during which it sounded as if a lot of kicking and biting was going on; then something broke free of the goblins and came zigzagging crazily through the air of the corridor and came to rest on Ellie's shoulder. It was larger than the sprite and looked more like a tiny human being, apart from its long thin fingers and spiky toes, all of which were gripping her T-shirt as if its life depended on it.

'How sweet!' the Dodman sneered. 'A Wildwood fairy come to pay its respects to the daughter of the Queen.'

The goblins came charging up to him.

'I found it!' cried Boggart.

'So what?' shrieked Bogie, shoving him sideways. 'I brought it: I want my reward!'

'You want a reward, do you, Bogie?'

The smaller of the two goblins nodded vigorously, and the sprite's red glow gleamed in Bogie's greedy eyes as he gazed adoringly up at his master.

'Give me the key.' One of the goblins relinquished it to the Dodman reluctantly. 'I think you *both* deserve a reward,' their master went on smoothly.

Boggart and Bogie exchanged a surprised glance, and grinned from ear to ear, which was a long way.

As fast as a striking snake, the Dodman's free hand shot out and smacked both creatures soundly around their ugly heads.

'There's your reward! That's what you deserve for your clumsiness! What's the point of capturing a fairy for me if you squabble over it and let it go? Dolts! Dullards! Dunces!'

He lashed out at them with his boot and they backed away, quivering. They knew what the dog-headed one could be like in one of his tempers. Poor old Batface had copped for it last week and he hadn't walked the same since.

'Take this, and hold it steady,' he told Grizelda, handing her the sprite.

'Then can I eat it?'

'No!' Ellie cried in horror. 'No, you can't!'

The Dodman regarded her curiously. Then he gave her a lopsided smile. 'Sweet . . . Well, maybe we won't let her eat it yet, if you behave, eh?'

He caught hold of her hair, wrapping a long hank of it around his fist, and pulled her head towards him. Ellie squirmed. 'Ow!'

Something glinted silver in the darkness; then suddenly there was a knife-blade before her face.

Ellie felt her knees go weak.

'No, please . . .'

She closed her eyes. There was a shearing sound, and abruptly her head was free of his grasp. Her eyes came open, to find the Dodman standing there before her with a knife in one hand and something dark and floppy in the other. Unconsciously, her hand went to her head.

'You cut my hair!'

'Be thankful it is only your hair, for the moment.' He stowed the knife away and caught up the fairy, detaching its tiny hands roughly from the fabric of Ellie's top. 'Listen to me,' he told it savagely. 'You will go back to your Wildwood and you will find Queen Isadora and show her this.' He wound the strand of hair around and around its slender body, making sure it did not interfere with the creature's wings. 'Tell her that I hold her daughter, Eleanor, hostage and that if she does not give herself up to me by full moon, the next gift I will send her will be a rather more painfully acquired part of her pretty Ellie, followed by another and another and another.' His grip tightened on the fairy until it cried out. 'Have you got that?'

The Wildwood fairy stared at the dog-headed man with its great violet eyes. 'This is a cruel thing you do, Dodman,' it said, and its voice was surprisingly low for such a small creature. It turned its head to regard Ellie. 'Forgive me, Princess. If I do not carry the message he will only find another to take my place . . .'

'She mustn't come!' Ellie cried. 'Tell her—'

One of the Dodman's hard elbows caught her in the ribs, sending her spinning backwards into the cell. She fell back against the hard bed, gasping for breath.

'Enough!'

The cell door banged shut, consigning Ellie to total darkness. The sound of muffled complaint came from outside, then the door cracked open and something small and pink and glowing came arcing through the black space. Then the door banged shut again.

CHAPTER ELEVEN

Trapped by a Troll

Iggy found himself staring up into quite the ugliest face he had ever seen in any of his nine lives. Under a shock of purple hair, it seemed to consist mainly of a mouth – a very large mouth containing a lot of long, sharp yellow teeth which stuck out at all sorts of angles – a hooked nose like the beak of some predatory bird, and a pair of bright, beady close-set eyes which were regarding him with an expression he recognised all too well.

Unadulterated greed.

'Help!'

What he had hoped would come out as a yowl that might be heard for miles emerged as a pathetic squeak, since his captor was holding him so tightly around the middle with its hard, horny claws that he could hardly draw breath.

The monster's mouth opened wider, emitting a terrible stench.

'Yum. Cat,' it said. 'Haven't eaten cat for ages. What a treat.'

It brought a squirming Iggy closer.

'Don't eat me,' Iggy pleaded. 'I'd taste awful.'

'Awful?' The monster's huge brow drew itself into a puzzled frown.

'Like . . .' Iggy searched for a comparison which might delay the inevitable. 'Like . . . old boots. I'm very scrawny, you see: there's not much meat on me at all. I'm all fur and bones . . .' Even getting this out was an effort. He hung there, panting and hoping.

'Old boots . . . Hmmm . . .' There was a pause as his captor thought about this. Then its eyes gleamed. 'I ate a pair of old boots once. Hundred-league boots. They belonged to a cat, as I recall. He was still in them at the time. Didn't taste that bad. A bit chewy. And the laces got caught between my teeth.' It paused. 'The whiskers did, too.'

Iggy stared at it aghast. 'You ate Puss-in-Boots?'

A horrible noise reverberated through the air, as if someone had just switched on a giant engine. Iggy gulped. Then he realised the monster was laughing.

'Silly cat. That was just a story!'

A long grey tongue came out of the huge mouth, like a serpent emerging from a cave. Iggy watched in horrified fascination as it travelled across the horrible teeth and lips, leaving a slick of silvery slobber behind. He could imagine that tongue savouring him. It made him shudder.

'*And* . . . I'm – er, poisonous!'

'Poisonous? Whoever heard of a poisonous cat?'

'I'd give you a terrible bellyache if you ate me. You'd be sick for weeks.'

'Sick? I'm never sick. My mother always said I had a very robust constitution.'

It was hard to imagine that such a beast could ever have had a mother.

'How . . . how is your mother?' Iggy asked in a desperate attempt to engage the thing in polite conversation.

'I ate her, too.'

'Oh.'

The vast rumble of the monster's laugh thrummed through Iggy's bones.

'You really think I ate my mother?'

'Yes . . . er, no.' Iggy felt like an idiot. This was hopeless. He braced himself. 'Look, if you're going to eat me, just get on and do it. All I'm saying is that you'll regret it.'

'Oh, I don't think so. Trolls aren't noted for their sense of regret.'

Iggy thought hard.

'Don't you live under bridges and eat goats? You know, like the three billy-goats Gruff?'

'Such a ridiculous story. You think I would let a nice juicy goat go safely on its way just because it said there was a bigger, tastier one coming along in a minute? You'd have to be pretty stupid to fall for that sort of trick.' It squinted suspiciously at Iggy. 'Do you think I'm stupid?'

'Of course not . . .'

'Of course not. Nah, I ate all three of them.' And the troll licked its lips as if reminiscing.

'There's a lot more meat on a goat than on a cat,' Iggy reminded it again. 'And my fur would get stuck in your throat.'

'Oh, I'd skin you first,' the troll said cheerfully. 'I'm not a complete heathen, you know. It's a bit of a faff, skinning a cat – I never bother with skinning rabbits, since even the biggest ones aren't much more than a morsel – but a cat's a different matter. Bit special. Once in a blue moon sort of thing. In fact, I think I've got some rather good cat recipes somewhere. There's Moggy Meringue: though I'm out of dinosaur eggs at the moment. And Kitty Casserole . . . no, too many vegetables in that one. Vegetables: can't bear the things. Mother always said they were good for me; but I reason that being good's not really appropriate for a troll. Epitome of "bad", don't you think? So eating things that are good for you might take the edge off being bad, and I can't really afford that, you know. But there was one special recipe that didn't involve any veg, as I recall. One of the witches on the Blasted Heath gave it to me, and they certainly never ate anything so boring as a vegetable. Now, what was it again?' It rolled its eyes, consulting its capacious memory. 'Ah, yes: eye of newt and toe of frog, tongue of dog and wool of bat, goes very nicely with a cat.'

Iggy regarded him dubiously. 'I don't think it would, you know.'

'Well, trial and error is what good cuisine is all about,' the troll declared cavalierly. 'I shall have a cast about in my larder and see what I can find to stuff you with – make a bit of a feast of it. Might even invite Grizelda over for dinner.' It thought about this for a moment. 'On second thoughts, perhaps not. She doesn't really appreciate gourmet food; and you are quite small. I'm not sure there would be enough to go around. A couple of legs apiece. Tail for one and head for the other . . .'

Iggy felt faint.

The troll's grip on him tightened.

'Hmmm . . . Decisions to make. Let's put you away some-where safe while I decide how I'm going to cook you, shall we?'

And he lumbered across the open ground to the entrance to a cave. Inside, there were a lot of big clay pots with lids on. With his free hand, the troll lifted one lid and peered inside. 'Fairies,' he said thoughtfully. 'Fairy mash, maybe, with a gar-nish of triffid and giant hogweed . . .' He replaced the lid with a clang and lifted the next one. 'Ah, selkie-flippers. A bit fishy with cat, I think . . .'

The next pot was empty.

'In you go, what did you say your name was?'

'I didn't.'

'Be like that, then. I always like to know the names of those I eat. Names are special: they have power. Mother said it was what made me big and strong. I dare say you'll tell me before too long.'

And he dropped Iggy into the pot. The lid shut out the light.

CHAPTER TWELVE

A Deception

Cernunnos returned as the sun came up over the Wildwood, tinting every leaf and branch with an ominous wash of pale-red light.

Darius looked up from his vigil beside the sleeping woman and her child. He knew at once that something was terribly wrong. The Lord of the Wildwood's face was grim.

The Horned Man put a finger to his lips and drew the centaur aside. 'Come with me,' he said softly.

'But who will watch over Queen Isadora and the Princess Alice?'

Cernunnos lifted his eyes to the dawn sky. Above them, two

dark shapes circled silently, wings outstretched, like a pair of buzzards quartering their territory.

'Dragons? Can we trust them? Their kind have not always proved loyal.'

'Xarkanadûshak and his lady will keep watch: they owe a debt to the boy, Ben, and his family.'

In the shadow of a huge oak, its bark gouged and twisted by the centuries, the Lord of the Wildwood showed the centaur what he held cradled. It was a fairy, and it lay in the crook of Cernunnos's arm in a daze, its eyes tight shut and its mouth down-turned in misery. Something dark and sleek had been wrapped around its narrow torso.

Darius stared at it, uncomprehending.

'It is as I feared,' Cernunnos said in a low voice. 'The Dodman has taken a hostage: and not just any hostage, but the daughter of the Queen herself.'

'Her daughter?' For a moment the Horse Lord's face clouded with bewilderment; then his eyes grew round. As if unable to help himself, he reached a hand towards the fairy, touched lightly the silken stuff around its body. 'Eleanor? They have taken the Princess Eleanor? And this . . .'

'. . . is her hair, yes. Sent to us by the Dodman as a token of her capture. He will send worse next time. He said he would send her back piece by piece . . .'

'Next time?' Darius echoed.

'If Isadora does not give herself up to him, by full moon.'

'But she cannot, she has only just returned to us. And full moon is only two days away . . .' But even as Darius said this, the image of a pretty dark-haired girl blushing at the Aldstane on the other side of the wild road floated before his eyes and his heart clenched inside him.

'Isadora cannot give herself up, no. We cannot allow her to become the Dodman's possession, and so she must not know of this.'

The centaur regarded the Lord of the Wildwood in horror. 'But we cannot keep such a secret from our Queen, it would not be right.'

'There are greater rights in the world, Darius. The girl is a small price to pay for the future safety of all Eidolon.' Cernunnos bent so that his antlered head cast a long shadow across the forest floor, and with his free hand scooped up a handful of fallen oak leaves, brown as nuts and crisp with frost. These he held out towards Darius, then let them filter through his fingers back to the soft ground. 'All things have their allotted span in the world. They live, they die, and they give themselves back to the cycle of Eidolon, so that others may live.' Between their feet, insects and worms moved where the leaves had been disturbed. A pair of eyes shone watchfully from the depths of a hole revealed in the roots of the old tree.

Darius swallowed his protest, though his brow was wrinkled by the turmoil of his thoughts.

As he struggled for words, the fairy stirred. It pushed itself upright and blinked.

'Can you get this stuff off me?' it pleaded, plucking at the hair.

Darius exchanged a glance with the Lord of the Wildwood,

who nodded. Then he stepped forward and with careful fingers unwound the hank of Ellie's hair from the creature. It tingled against his palm like a live thing. He felt tears prick his eyes.

'What will he do to her?'

Cernunnos firmed his jaw. 'Nothing, if we get to her first.'

The Horse Lord's chin came up with a start. 'You mean, we might rescue her?' he asked with sudden hope.

'That, or aid her on her way to silence.'

'You cannot mean—'

'Hush. I pray that it will not come to that. But let us speak no more of this now. There are many ears in the forest and not all of them are loyal to our cause.'

'But what about the messenger?' Darius regarded the fairy with concern.

'There is no need to talk about me as if I am deaf, or stupid, or absent,' the creature said crossly. 'I did not ask to be captured by the Dodman; and I certainly did not ask to have to carry such a horrid message, nor have that hair tied around me. It was pretty hard to fly with all that stuff on, I can tell you.'

Cernunnos looked down at the fairy. 'You did well, Nettle Blueflower,' he said gently. 'And now you must recuperate. I will send you with Beechnut and Quickthorn to the southern edge of the wood. Make sure you stay there until you are well.'

'But I'm already feeling better,' the fairy called Nettle Blueflower protested. 'I'm sure I'll be fine after a short nap.'

'Even so,' the Lord of the Wildwood reiterated, 'it is my wish that you should travel south.' And he summoned the two escorts, passed Nettle into their care, and he and the centaur watched as the trio flew slowly away, Beechnut and Quickthorn supporting the messenger carefully between them.

'I cannot risk him talking,' Cernunnos explained softly. 'If this news leaks out too early it could be disastrous.'

Darius transferred his intent gaze to the stag-headed man. 'And they are truly taking him south? He will come to no harm?'

The Lord of the Wildwood regarded him curiously, and a shadow passed before his peat-brown eyes. 'Do you really believe I would bring deliberate harm to one of my subjects?' he asked.

Darius looked at the ground, feeling ashamed for questioning the Lord of the Wildwood. But there was still the matter of the Princess Eleanor, and he made a solemn promise to himself that he would do whatever was in his power to save her.

'My lady, I trust you are well rested?'

As the shadow of the Horned Man fell across her, Isadora opened her eyes. In the rosy light of dawn they shone the startling green of the buds on a spring larch. A night in the Secret Country had rejuvenated her.

She sat up and looked around. Baby Alice lay cradled in the nest of moss and clothes where she had laid her in the night, sleeping peacefully, forehead to forehead with her piglet-doll.

Isadora smiled. 'I am well, Lord Cernunnos.' Then she frowned, remembering. 'Did you manage to save the poor soul whom the Wild Hunt were pursuing?'

'Alas no, my lady. The Gabriel Hounds were well away

before we could reach them.' It was an evasion, though not precisely a lie.

Isadora looked pained. She got to her feet, brushing leaf mould and dust from her skirts. 'I cannot bear that such acts are carried out in my realm without opposition. We must do something to rescue the unfortunate captive. Tell me, Lord Cernunnos, how many of my folk have taken the Dodman's side against us?'

The Lord of the Wildwood shook his head. 'It is not just that he has gathered a horde of creatures to him, my lady, but that many have come to be born into Eidolon with no knowledge of anything but the ways of terror: our greater task will be to persuade them that there is still hope in the world, that the future can be better for us all if they resist him and come over to us. But . . .' he hesitated.

'Go on.'

'We are weak, my Queen. Magic has been leached out of Eidolon systematically by the Dodman's actions. He has stolen our folk out of this world and allowed them to fail and die in the Other World. And he has killed many and broken the spirits of more. Greed and laziness have claimed many souls. As we grow weaker, so he grows stronger, or so it seems; and the sum total of magic has dwindled. There will be less power for you to draw on now; and fewer to call to your banner, too.'

'What are you saying, Cernunnos? That I have been away too long and that it is now too late to save my people?'

'No, my Queen: never that. But we are not ready yet to take him on in open war.'

'So we must allow whichever poor creature was taken by his hounds to languish and die without our aid?'

'I fear we are not yet ready to storm Corbenic Castle.'

Isadora's gentle face became grim. 'Then we must find another way.'

Darius stepped forward. 'I pledge myself to the task of rescuing the captive, my Queen. I shall not rest until she is rescued.'

'She?' The Queen's gaze became sharp as glass. 'So you know who the captive is, then?'

The centaur shuffled his hooves under her scrutiny and the disapproving glare of Cernunnos. But just as she was about to question him further, there was a great deal of splashing and shouting from behind them, and Baby Alice awoke with a start and began to howl. Isadora scooped her up and walked back towards the stream to see what all the fuss was about.

A group of woodland folk had emerged from their dens and secret places and were braving the daylight to line the banks where the waters cascaded down into a sunlit plunge-pool. In the middle of this, looking rather wet and flustered, floated her husband, in a soaking anorak, with an umbrella held aloft – though if it had been meant to keep the worst of the waterfall off him, it hadn't worked. Two nymphs caught hold of the anorak and started to tow him to the shore, where they hauled him up unceremoniously and left him there like a beached seal.

'Clive!'

Mr Arnold blinked and stared up at where his wife stood

with Baby Alice cradled in her arms, shaking her head in disbelief, her hair made numinous by the sun. All he could make out was her silhouette, but it was a shape he recognised, in this world or any other.

'Isadora, my darling . . .'

Behind him, in the shallows, Ben watched this exchange with rising dread. In a moment he would have to tell his mother what had happened to her accident-prone family since they had last been together. It was bad enough that his father was here, and ill; but he knew the world would change shape as soon as he told her about Ellie. He turned to the old mermaid.

'Thank you, Melusine,' he said. He paused as a thought suddenly struck him. 'You don't know my friend, Silver, do you?'

The mermaid considered this. 'Silver . . . Silver . . .' She shook her head and water droplets sprayed all around and fell like rain. 'No, I don't think I recall that name.'

'She's a selkie,' Ben added.

'Oh, selkies,' Melusine said dismissively. 'Unreliable folk, selkies. They're only part-timers. Haven't got the same commitment or the stamina of us true mermaids. Really, if you're going to be something in life you should be that one thing and stick to it, I say, rather than chopping and changing all the time.'

'Maybe you knew her father – He Who Hangs Around on the Great South Rock to Attract Females?'

For a moment a huge grin lit the old mermaid's face. 'Now *him* I remember! Skerry, we called him. When he transformed, he was a real beauty: tallest man I ever saw, with a mop of wild blond hair and eyes the colour of a summer sky. And he had a daughter, you say?'

Ben nodded, trying to remember Silver's true name. Then it came to him like a flash of light in the head, and he could see her in his mind's eye in her girl-form, with her skin as pale as moonlight and her long hair clinging to her shoulders, and he smiled. 'She Who Swims the Silver Path of the Moon,' he said happily.

The mermaid regarded him curiously. 'I don't know her, my dear: but you obviously do, because you're blushing like a wood-sprite!' She cackled. 'Well, if she takes after her father she'll be a pretty thing for sure, so no wonder you're smitten.'

Smitten? Ben blushed even harder. Ridiculous. He didn't even like girls. But, said a little voice at the back of his head, unhelpfully, she wasn't a girl, at least not half the time.

'Ben?'

His mother's eyebrows shot up in surprise. Then she waved to him from the far side of the pool.

'I have to go,' he said to the old mermaid. 'Perhaps I'll see you again.'

The crone laughed. 'Not if I see you first, laddie,' she said. 'You're lucky I didn't sing you down to my lair the last time.' And she winked at him and dived out of sight, leaving Ben feeling rather bemused and even more anxious than he had felt before. Was everything in the Secret Country so scary? He waded out of the water towards his mother; but before he could reach her, a shadow fell across him.

He looked up. It was the Horned Man.

Cernunnos offered him a hand up out of the stream, and he grasped it. It felt hard and dry and warm, smooth as polished wood. The fingers tightened minutely. 'Ben,' the stag-headed man started quietly, pulling the boy on to dry land, 'you will say nothing about Eleanor to your mother.' His grip tightened.

Ben stared at him. 'I won't?'

'You will not. She must not know, not yet. It is too dangerous.'

'But Dad knows.'

'Your father is sleeping.'

The Horned Man pointed to where Mr Arnold lay cocooned in the pile of blankets and clothes recently vacated by Baby Alice. His eyes were closed and he looked as if he was dreaming, for a huge smile was on his face.

'He will not wake up again until I allow it,' Cernunnos said. 'It is for his own good as much as for any other reason: he should not be here, as you should know.' He fixed Ben with a stern gaze.

'I couldn't stop him,' Ben said defensively. 'I mean, I tried to, but he is my dad . . .'

'You must rescue your sister Eleanor from the clutches of the Dodman,' Cernunnos told him. 'And you must tell no one. Darius will go with you.'

'But . . . I can't lie to Mum. She always knows.'

The centaur appeared at Cernunnos's shoulder.

'Then we must go now,' Darius said simply, and reaching

down, he caught hold of Ben and swung him up on to his back. Before Ben could utter a word of protest they were galloping away through the trees.

Mrs Arnold watched them go with a puzzled expression on her face. Then she strode up to Cernunnos, looking very determined. 'Where is Darius going with my son?'

Cernunnos turned to her. 'I gather the Wanderer came after me and did not return,' he said smoothly.

'I sent him, yes.' Isadora frowned. 'He really should have been back by now.'

'I am sure they will find him and bring him back shortly. But in the meantime, I must ask you: did you bring the Book of Naming with you?'

She nodded. 'Of course.'

'Excellent!' The Lord of the Wildwood's eyes gleamed. 'Then we have him! We can Name our army at our will. The dinosaurs and dragons will have him out of Corbenic in no time. We shall drag him in chains across Eidolon, make an example of him before all the doubters. We shall extinguish the lives of those who have taken his side. We can show no mercy, or they will think us weak—'

'Cernunnos, stop.' The Queen's face was pale, but her eyes were aflame with green fire. 'We shall do no such thing. There has been too much coercion and violence in this world since I have been away, and I cannot condone more wickedness!'

'Wickedness?' Shadows passed across the stag-headed man's face like storm clouds. 'Wickedness?' His voice began to boom so that his antlers rattled and shook. 'The wickedness in your kingdom comes from the Dodman. He has been stealing your folk, selling them, killing them, torturing them, taking their magic from them. We need to Name our allies and make a stand.'

'I will not compel anyone to our cause.'

Cernunnos stared at her in disbelief. 'But you have the Book of Naming,' he pointed out slowly, as if to someone rather stupid. 'You can summon them and then use your magic to compel them to your will. It's what the Dodman has been doing with the magic he's managed to extract from your hapless subjects!'

'The Book is an ancient volume which records and honours the true names of our folk,' Isadora said gently. 'It is not a tool for war and I will not use it as such. I will not misuse the magic of Eidolon as my enemy has done: it would make me as bad as him, and then to whom would the good folk of Eidolon look for guidance? No, we must persuade them to join our cause freely. It will require their courage and a difficult choice which they must make for themselves. I have been away too long to expect to command their loyalty.'

'Persuade? That will take time: too much time!'

'Then we had better make a start,' the Queen said softly, laying a gentling hand on his arm. 'I will call them by their true Names, but I will not compel them, do you understand me?'

The Lord of the Wildwood held her gaze for several long, defiant moments. Then he sighed. 'You are our Queen, despite all the years that you have been away.'

Together they crossed the sward to the suitcase and Isadora

brought out the battered old leatherbound volume and opened it up. Where in the Other World its pages had seemed to a casual glance empty and unmarked, here they swirled into colourful life, offering a glorious confusion of pictures and script. Here, there was listed the true name of every one of Eidolon's creatures. The names came mysteriously into existence as soon as each new life came into the world; and faded just as mysteriously when a life was snuffed out. There were a lot of blank spaces amongst the pages now: far more than there should be from natural causes.

Isadora began to turn the pages back, past 'Dragons and Dinosaurs' towards 'Sprites, Sylphs and Small People' when the heading 'Humans, Witches, Trolls and Elvenfolk' stopped her in her tracks. There, in splendid living colour, were tiny portraits of herself, her wicked brother, Awful Cousin Cynthia; and of Ellie, Ben and Alice.

The Lord of the Wildwood peered over the Queen's shoulder. He scanned the book curiously. Then his features sharpened. 'I wonder . . .' he said.

He took the Book from her and riffled through the leaves. Then he frowned and started his search again.

'That's strange . . .'

'What are you looking for?'

Cernunnos flicked another page open. 'He must be here somewhere,' he muttered.

The Queen smiled tiredly. 'Did you really think I hadn't thought of that?' she said. 'Searching for the Dodman's true name was the first thing I did. He's not in there.'

'But that's impossible.'

'Apparently not.'

'But all the creatures of Eidolon are in the Book.'

'Apart from him. Odd, isn't it? It's puzzled me for a long time.'

The Lord of the Wildwood sighed. 'It seems there are no easy solutions to our dilemma. We'd better make a start with our summons of the small creatures, then. Their movements will be less evident for the Dodman's spies to detect, and we can better shelter them here until we are ready to move against him.'

CHAPTER THIRTEEN

Spies

'And you say the Dodman has captured the Princess Eleanor?'

'Yesss, mistressss. He holds her in the dungeonsss at the cassstle.'

'Excellent! I shall be Queen soon enough at this rate. The Dodman will kill Ellie, and Isadora will die in the war that must soon come, and then I shall claim the throne.'

The creature who in the Other World was known to Ben and Ellie as Awful Cousin Cynthia cackled gleefully and, making a fist, thrust one clawed hand into the air in a gesture of triumph.

'And what about Ben and the Baby Alisssse?'

'Ah, Ben. I have plans for Ben,' Cynthia declared cheerfully. 'And even a scrawny creature like you could probably deal with a baby.'

The Sphynx had no hackles, for it had no fur, but the little ridges of loose skin around its neck flexed in irritation at this remark. If it had had whiskers, they would have bristled.

'Besides,' Cynthia went on breezily, 'no one would accept a baby as a queen; I've read my history books. They'd appoint a regent, or a regentess – someone to take care of the land while the little beast grew up. If it ever did.' She held a hand out in front of her and admired it, though it was hard to see what there was to admire, for it was covered in scales and ended in long, horny claws the colour of a fresh bruise.

In fact, it would have been hard for Ben and Ellie to recognise their cousin, for a strange and terrible trans-formation had taken place as soon as she crossed between worlds. Here, she was hunchbacked and spiky-nosed – as spiteful-looking on the outside as they knew her to be on the inside. Only her shock of orange hair remained the same; that, and her pale-green gooseberry eyes, mean elbows, and her delight in tormenting things smaller and more vulnerable than herself. At the moment she was sitting on a log, holding a small greenish-grey fairy, which was mewing as pathetically as a newborn kitten. The Sphynx regarded the fairy with interest. It hoped that when Cynthia had finished with the fairy, it might make a tasty snack. It watched curiously as Cynthia did something which was followed by a soft ripping sound. The fairy screamed. Cynthia examined the tiny, transparent wings thoughtfully, holding them up to the weak wintry sun.

'Hmmm,' she said. 'These would make great earrings.'

She cast the damaged fairy down roughly, where it fell amongst a knot of three or four others in a similar condition. They made a space for it, and one of the larger ones put its arms around it to offer whatever comfort can be offered to a creature which can no longer do the thing it was born to do: fly joyously through the Wildwood like the very embodiment of magic.

The Sphynx stalked over to the group and assessed them with its angled amber eyes. It did not think it could eat them all at once, but it probably wouldn't have to seek food for another two days.

Cynthia grabbed its ratlike tail. 'Go and get me some more,' she demanded. 'No, wait. I'm bored with fairies. What about a baby dragon? The hide would make a fabulous handbag!'

The Sphynx gave her a flat stare. Taking its time, it stretched out its front legs, then its back legs, then arched its back into a tight parabola. 'I think not, mistressss. Even the babies are dangerousss; and their parentsss are edgy already. They know the Queen isss here, and they await developmentssss, very alert, very watchful. What about a nice sprite; or a pretty little sylph?'

Cynthia clapped her hands together. 'A wood-sylph! A wood-sylph! Yes, yes, yes! I can pull its hair out and braid it into golden chains.'

Muttering darkly to itself, the Sphynx cast a last, lingering, mournful look at the discarded fairies and stalked off into the undergrowth. Sylphs came in all sorts of sizes and could be tricky to catch. Also, the bigger ones tended to keep the little ones hidden away. But it knew where it could find some, left defenceless by the depredations of another of Eidolon's monsters. *Oh yesss*, it knew.

'It isss not right, it isss not fair, that she should treat me so. I who am the descendant of Kingsss,' the Sphynx growled to itself as it trod the fallen leaves of the Wildwood. It gnashed its sharp little teeth in frustration. 'But I will have my due one day, when she isss Queen. Then I shall have my pick of all the lovely fairiesss, and the little mermaids, and the sprites, too. I shall have a troop of banshees to scare them out of the trees and into my clawsss! I shall eat only the tastiest pieces, and throw the rest away for the goblinsss to squabble over.'

It could imagine this fine future now, without much effort. There would be a bed of red velvet close – but not too close – to the fire in the great hall; and the Gabriel Hounds would be kept chained safely out of the way in the courtyard. Unless it could persuade Cynthia to have them put to death . . .

But just how might one kill the ghost-dogs? If they were ghosts, then by definition they were already dead; and it is hard to kill something that is already dead.

And then there was the Dodman, too.

Maybe she will kill him, too, it thought, suddenly hopeful.

It paused in mid-step.

'Yesss, once she hasss claimed the throne, she will not need him any more.'

Its eyes closed in pleasure. It was still purring to itself at this delightful thought when something grabbed it hard by the scruff of the neck, quite without warning, and swung it up into the air.

'And who is this miscreant?'

Darius turned to dangle the kicking captive in front of Ben's nose.

Ben stared at it. 'That's the Sphynx,' he said. 'I doubt it's up to any good.'

The hairless beast turned its cold yellow gaze upon him. 'Good is for losersss,' it hissed, twisting suddenly in the centaur's grip.

But Darius was too quick and too ready for it. 'Oh, no you don't, little spy,' he told it, clutching its scrawny body even more fiercely. 'I've heard too many tales of the poor creatures you've caught and killed in our Wildwood.'

Ben regarded the Sphynx with loathing. 'What shall we do with it?'

'Turn it over to Cernunnos,' the centaur said grimly.

At this, the spy cringed. Its mouth trembled. 'Don't do that,' it wheedled. 'He'll crush me between his hard hands like an egg. He's cruel, the Horned One: cruel and pitiless.'

'The Lord of the Wildwood is ever fair,' Darius returned. 'But I grant he will not look kindly on one who has pitilessly hurt and betrayed his folk.'

'I was made to do it!' the Sphynx cried. 'There is never any peace from either of them and their endless demands—'

It stopped in a rush, its eyes darting here and there in panic, realising it had said more than it should.

'Them? Who do you mean by "them"?' Darius cried.

'Well, Awful Cousin Cynthia, for one,' Ben said. 'It's her cat, after all. As for the other: well, I bet it's spying for the Dodman, too. I'd bet it knows plenty about what goes on at the castle.'

He slipped from the centaur's broad back and came around to give the hairless cat a hard stare.

'What about my sister, Ellie?' he asked furiously. 'Have you seen her?'

'Oh, yessss. I've seen her.'

'Where is she? Do you know where the Dodman has taken her?'

But the Sphynx's gaze became unreadable, flat-lidded. 'I know many thingsss,' it said cryptically. It paused, then winked unpleasantly. 'I know, for example, what has become of your friend, the Wanderer . . .'

'Iggy?' Ben was horrified. 'What do you mean, "what has become" of him?'

'Make the horse-boy let me go,' the Sphynx teased, 'and I'll tell you what I know.'

But Darius shook the captive hard. 'Tell us what you know now or I will break your scrawny neck myself!'

Ben turned anguished eyes upon the centaur. 'Has something happened to Iggy?' There had been no sign of his friend in the woodland clearing where the mermaid had taken them down the stream and the waterfall to find his mother, but he hadn't thought anything of it at the time.

Darius looked uncomfortable. 'Your mother sent him off

after Cernunnos to find out who it was the Wild Hunt were pursuing. He never returned.'

Ben felt as if his heart might stop. This news was even harder to bear than that of his sister's capture, for the Dodman would surely never kill Ellie, whereas anything might have happened to the little black-and-brown cat who despite all his apparent toughness and absurd gravelly voice really was quite hopeless when left to his own devices.

'Is he hurt?' he asked the Sphynx desperately.

The Sphynx gave him an evil grin. 'Oh, he's probably more than hurt by now.'

And that, no matter how much Darius threatened the hairless cat, or how much Ben cajoled it, was all the Sphynx would say.

Ben walked off to one side to think. He sat down. He closed his eyes. But nothing came to him. It was as if someone had spring-cleaned his brain and left it all shiny and tidy inside, but completely useless.

'Oh, Iggy,' he whispered to himself. 'What if I never see you again, my friend? Oh, Ignatius—' He clapped his hands over his mouth and leapt up. 'Hold your hands tight over the Sphynx's ears!' he told the centaur urgently. 'Make sure it can't hear anything.'

Looking puzzled, Darius did as he was asked.

Ben took a deep breath, then called into the chilly air:

'Ignatius Sorvo Coromandel – if you can hear me, come to me now!'

It was Iggy's true name, and as such gave Ben the power to

summon him three times, wherever he might be in this world or the next.

The shout echoed off the wintry trees and evaporated into the cold afternoon sky just like the vapour of Ben's breath. The centaur raised his head as if listening. They waited. And waited.

After a little while Darius shifted his grip on the Sphynx, which twitched its ears and stared at each of them suspiciously.

But nothing happened. Nothing at all.

Ignatius Sorvo Coromandel!

It came as if from a great distance – a thought more than a sound; like something in a dream; or an irritation at the back of the skull, like an itch he could not scratch.

Iggy had experienced this sensation before. Then, he had been chilling out on the shores of the Western Sea, watching the sun go down with a very pretty six-toed Jamaican Cat it had taken him three days' solid work to get close to; and he had not been at all pleased to hear the summons, which had dragged him halfway across Eidolon, through countless wild roads, a number of very scratchy bushes, across a wide moat (and everyone knew how much cats hated even a drop of water, let alone a whole lake of the stuff), past the snapping jaws of the Gabriel Hounds, and right into the clutches of the Dodman. And if that had not been bad enough, worse humiliation had followed.

Being flown through the air in a frilly bonnet drawn by a dozen struggling wood-sprites – all complaining about just how much some animals must eat in order to get to be so terribly heavy – had not been his finest hour. It made him blush (under-neath his fur) even to think of it.

But right now, trapped in a clay pot in the larder of a very large, very ugly and very hungry troll, he had never been so happy to hear a summons in his life. The problem was, he couldn't seem to do anything about it. The lid was heavy and firmly attached, and no amount of rolling around or kicking out would get the jar to topple over. He knew: he'd been trying for hours.

But it gave him new hope that someone, somewhere in one of the worlds, cared enough about him to call him by his true name. He thought it was Ben, though the voice was muffled and distant. But then the significance of this struck him, and he thought: if Ben is calling me, he must be in trouble!

This gave him the energy to kick harder again at the inside of the pot, but still it did not budge an inch.

Iggy sat back down, panting with the effort. He could not help himself, and he could not help his friend. He was truly a sorry excuse for a cat. He sat, head down, contemplating his feet in the darkness, and listened to the sound of his heartbeat echo-ing off the heavy clay walls of his prison, imagining the sort of dishes a troll might make out of him – like Cat-in-the-Hole or Moggy Meatballs or Kitten Nuggets; or even simply Fillet of Feline and Frog Fries – until a thought penetrated the thick clouds of self-pity swirling around his brain.

'Idiot!' he proclaimed himself. 'Iggy, you're an idiot!'

He wasn't the first to have made this observation, not by a long chalk. There had been his father – Polo Horatio

Coromandel – on several occasions, and his tutor Henry 'the Navigator' Longshanks, who'd tried to teach him the finer points of star-gazing (in which he had failed miserably); and countless others before and since. He'd begun to think they'd been right all along; but perhaps now was the time to prove them wrong.

He took a deep, deep breath, closed his eyes, and yowled as hard as he could: '*BENJAMIN CHRISTOPHER ARNOLD!*'

CHAPTER FOURTEEN

The Troll

Ben was so surprised he almost fell over.

'Did you hear that?' he asked the centaur.

Darius frowned. 'Hear what?'

But Ben was already running, as if dragged by an invisible rope.

'Hey!' the Horse Lord shouted. 'Wait for me!' And he gathered up his heels and galloped after the fast-disappearing boy, with the Sphynx yowling loudly in his fist.

Ben had not known he could run so fast: in fact, he wasn't entirely sure this sort of running had much to do with him at all. If he'd been able to run like this in the Other

World he'd have been a bit of a sports star at school, which he most definitely was not. But despite the exhilaration of being able to move so fast, it was a bit difficult keeping your eyes open for obstacles. Tree roots kept trying to trip him up, and rabbit-holes – or holes where something rather larger than rabbits (he didn't like to imagine what) lived – kept trying to swallow his feet. After a few minutes of the relentless concentration it was taking to stay upright and without a broken neck, he was both breathless and exhausted. He had a stitch in one side under his ribs and his muscles were complaining at being used for exercise they weren't accustomed to. He wanted to stop – or at least slow down – but something wouldn't let him. It was not just the insistent voice reverberating around his head, calling his name over and over again, like a distant echo of the summons; but a physical sensation too, as if someone else entirely now had charge of his body.

And now ahead of him there loomed a considerable obstacle: a dense expanse of bramble and thorn. But even though he could see it coming at him, he didn't seem to be able to avoid it or even slow down.

'Darius!' he cried. 'Help!'

He couldn't even turn his head, let alone diverge from his course. The thicket loomed up at him, spiky and destructive, without showing any sign of a gap or pathway into which he could dive. Some of the thorns were an inch long or more; some were covered with snagged swatches of wool or fur; and he could have sworn some were stained an ominous red. He closed his eyes, even though the thin film of his lids felt like scant protection, and waited for the impact.

The next thing he knew, there was a drumming of hooves behind him, a shout of warning, and then a strong arm encircled his waist and whisked him off his feet and Ben found himself sitting astride the centaur's broad back once more. He breathed a huge sigh of relief.

'Thanks!'

'Here,' said the Horse Lord, veering to a halt alongside the thicket. He thrust the Sphynx at Ben. 'Take this creature and hold it tight. Keep one hand firm on the scruff of its neck and it should stop struggling so much. It's a cat-thing: a reflex from the days when they were kittens and their mother picked them up like that.'

It was hard to believe the Sphynx had ever been a kitten, Ben thought: it looked as if it had come into the world as ugly as Yoda and as evil as it was now. He held it hard under one arm, with his fist clutched in the loose skin of its neck, and although it gave him a gaze that was full of hatred, it didn't seem to be able to bite him or do anything worse.

'Now: why on Eidolon did you take off like that?'

'Iggy called me. It's some sort of magical summons. It's still pulling at me now.' Even so, he dug his free hand into Darius's mane in case he was suddenly dragged off.

The centaur nodded knowingly. 'Ah,' he said. 'That explains that, then.' He paused. 'You told him your true name?'

Ben nodded.

'That was unwise. You should never give out your true name except to those you would trust with your life.'

'I do trust Iggy with my life!' Ben returned hotly.

'Even so,' the centaur said, 'it is dangerous to give another such power over you: imagine what the Dodman would do with such knowledge.'

Ben shivered. 'I'm *never* giving *him* my true name,' he said.

'He will know it sssoon, anyway,' the Sphynx hissed. 'And then you will be at his mercy.' It laughed: a high, thin sound more like the cry of a creature in pain than an expression of mirth. 'Not that he has any!'

'What do you mean?'

But the hairless cat merely blinked enigmatically.

Ben gave it a hard stare, then transferred his gaze to the Horse Lord. 'Darius, we must rescue Iggy.'

'What about your sister? That was the task Cernunnos charged us with, not haring around trying to find your scatter-brained friend.'

'I know,' Ben said through gritted teeth. 'But I won't be able to do anything until I've fulfilled the summons: as soon as I'm on the ground again, I'll be racing off into that thicket. It's hard enough staying on your back as it is: it's like getting pulled by a huge magnet.'

'Magnet?' The centaur furrowed its brow.

'Don't you know about magnetic forces?' Ben asked, amazed.

Darius shook his head.

'Well . . .' Ben scoured his memory for what they had been

taught at school about the scientific principle of attraction and repulsion, but all he could remember with any real clarity was how he and Adam had dropped their magnets into a big barrel of iron filings so that they came out like giant furry caterpillars. 'Well, never mind about that,' he said quickly. 'Apart from anything else, Iggy is my friend and I won't rest until I've found him. Then we can go and help Ellie.'

The centaur sighed. The will of these humans from the Other World was strong. But perhaps it was just such strength and loyalty that was required to combat the forces which stood against Eidolon. 'All right, then, but if your friend is somewhere beyond this thicket then we have a bit of a problem.'

'What sort of problem?'

Darius sighed again. 'You'll see soon enough.'

And he did. The centaur took a roundabout route which skirted the thicket between the slender trunks of a birch wood, then tracked in amongst a series of outcrops which ended in a cliff in which a large cave stood like a great black mouth. Bones were scattered all around the entrance to the cave – bones and feathers and bits of fur.

Aghast, Ben scanned the area for the unwanted sight of any chunks of black-and-brown fur; but there was none to be seen. There was, however, an awful smell and a cloud of vapour, amidst which a large dark shape could be discerned, bending over a steaming pot.

Darius came to a silent halt. Ben opened his mouth to say something, then suddenly found himself pulled from the centaur's back by an unseen force, and his feet took him straight towards the misty shape.

'Ben, no!'

Ben heard the whispered warning, but there was nothing he could do about it. Within seconds he had entered the foul-smelling cloud of steam. The Sphynx wriggled desperately beneath his arm, but he held on to it.

'Adder's fork and blind-worm's sting,' a loud voice boomed out, and a huge shadowy figure threw something into a huge cauldron, which made it bubble and froth in a most disturbing way. The figure prodded them down with a long ladle, then squinted at the list in its hand. 'What's this? Lizard's leg and howlet's wing. Howlet? Those witches have the most atrocious handwriting. Must mean owlet, baby owl. I'm sure I've got one somewhere . . .'

It bustled off towards the cave.

Ben watched the thing move away, with the hair on the back of his neck standing on end. Whatever was it? It was huge! But he couldn't even turn around to look at it, for no matter what he wanted to do, his eyes were drawn to the cauldron. He stared at it in horror. Surely Iggy couldn't be in there? But the compulsion was drawing him towards the bubbling pot. With his heart in his mouth, he approached it. But the summons carried him past the cauldron to an area where a pile of utensils and jars had been piled in a higgledy-piggledy fashion. He found himself reaching out to a particularly large jar . . .

'Hello, what have we here? A visitor? And a complete oddity at that. Can't say I've ever seen anything like you before.

Though, come to think of it, you do have a look of Grizelda to you. She's much prettier than you are, though . . .'

The thing stepped into his field of vision.

Ben stared at it open-mouthed. He had never seen anything like it. For a start, it had noxious green skin, a ridiculous quiff of purple hair, and it was even taller than the Dodman.

'Don't worry, laddie: I haven't turned cannibal.' It paused, then leered at him. 'Yet.'

'Cannibal? But I'm not . . .' He faltered, not knowing what it was.

'A troll?' The thing roared with laughter. 'Well, we may not look much alike, laddie, but believe me, we're kissing cousins.'

Ben screwed his face up in disgust. He didn't much like kissing anyone, and he certainly didn't fancy kissing a troll. Still, it was a relief that it wasn't going to eat him. He watched in trepidation as it reached over and dropped whatever it had in its hand into the bubble and froth of the giant pot.

'Scale of dragon, tooth of wolf. Yes, yes, that's excellent. Now then, where's the main ingredient?'

The troll turned and lifted the lid off the big jar and withdrew something small and dark and kicking.

'Ben! Help me!'

Ben's mouth fell open in shock. Then: 'Iggy!' he gasped.

'Oh goodie,' said the troll, 'you know its name. That'll put a bit of power in the casserole.' He bent and picked up a big, sharp knife. 'Now then, you hold it down and I'll skin it. Can't abide the fur, though it's a mucky task having to get it off.'

'No!' cried Ben. 'No, you can't: he's my friend.'

'Friend?' The troll wrinkled its big knobbly brow. 'What's that, then, a friend?'

Ben had to think about that one. At last he said, 'Someone you spend time with, and laugh and have fun with.'

Still the troll looked puzzled.

'Someone you care about, and who cares about you?'

'Nope, no one I can think of,' it said. It thought for a moment. Did Grizelda count? It shook its head rather sadly. Not really.

'Someone you'd count on to help you if you're in a spot of trouble—'

'Like now?' Iggy rasped. He eyed the knife in the troll's hand nervously. '*Now* would be a very good time.'

From under Ben's arm there came a wheezing sound, like a squeezed bagpipe. 'Hee hee hee.'

A sudden thought struck Ben. He wasn't sure it was very ethical, but friendship was friendship . . . 'Tell you what,' he said to the troll, 'I'll do you a swap. I'll trade you this cat here for that rather furry one.' He dangled the Sphynx in front of the monster.

The Sphynx wriggled and spat and tried to rake Ben with its claws, but he held on tight.

Meanwhile, the troll peered at it dubiously. 'Are you sure that's a cat?' it asked. 'It looks more like a rat to me: a big rat, but a rat all the same.'

'Oh yes,' said Ben triumphantly. 'It's a hairless cat: you won't even need to skin it: it's a ready-meal!'

The troll stuck the skinning knife back into the woodblock

and held out its hand to Ben. Ben stared at the hand cautiously. It was massive and hairy and green and scaly, and the nails were all black and broken. He wondered what you might catch from a troll . . .

'Well, come on then,' the troll said impatiently. 'Shake on the bargain. Don't they teach you any manners where you come from?'

Tentatively, Ben extended his free hand and watched as it was engulfed by the troll's massive mitt. The troll shook his hand so hard that Ben's feet came off the ground and he nearly fell over. The next thing he knew, the Sphynx was in the troll's grasp and every single one of Iggy's claws was digging into the skin of Ben's chest and arm. Then the little black-and-brown cat burrowed his head under Ben's armpit and trembled all over.

'It's all right, Iggy,' Ben reassured him over and over, and at last Iggy withdrew his head and stared up at him with huge amber eyes. Then he braced himself.

'Thank you, Ben,' he growled. 'Of course I had my own plan of escape. But,' it gazed at the struggling Sphynx as the troll poised it over the bubbling pot, 'I like yours a lot better! That was a clever move!'

Ben blushed: partly with happiness, and partly with embarrassment – it hadn't really been a plan, as such. Besides, he couldn't help but feel bad for the Sphynx. Although it was such a horrid little sneaking beast, it was still a living creature and did not deserve to die in a troll's vile stew.

But even as he walked back towards the watching centaur, a shriek split the air.

'*Cynthia Lucrezia Creepie!*'

In the direst of straits, the Sphynx had summoned its mistress.

Darius hauled Ben on to his back. 'I do not think we want to stay around here to find out what happens next, do you?' he asked, indicating a small dark shape in the sky above them. Something up there was circling, and beginning to dive. Before either Ben or Iggy could answer, he broke into a swift canter which took them on a zigzag path between the slender silver birches away from the troll's den.

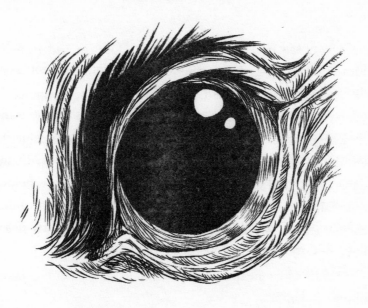

CHAPTER FIFTEEN

Ellie

In the confines of the stinking, windowless cell it was impossible to tell whether it was day or night. Ellie sat on the hard bed with her hands clasped together so tightly her knuckles hurt. She was shaking all over, for fear of the dark shadows and what might be hiding in them. If she moved, they would know she was there. So she sat still as a stone, trying not to cry: it wouldn't do to give Old Dogbreath that satisfaction.

Acorn the sprite clung to the edge of the bucket which the Dodman had so sarcastically referred to as her 'ensuite bathroom'. For a time, his pale-red light had illuminated details she really didn't want to think about, let alone see. He hadn't been very talkative: in fact, after the Dodman had thrown him into the dungeon after her, he'd barely said a word, as if he blamed her for his woeful fate. The only thing he had said, which had not been exactly cheering, was: 'Deep cells. Where they keep the dangerous ones.' It had looked at her hard with its strange little raspberry eyes and then asked, 'Are you dangerous?' And when Ellie had shaken her head and said no, not really, the sprite had nodded solemnly, then taken up its current stance, well out of reach, as if it did not really believe her.

After a while the sprite's light began to fade, plunging them into total darkness.

'Oh!' cried Ellie. 'Oh, don't go out!'

'Not going anywhere,' came back the tiny, scratchy voice. 'Imprisoned here. Just like you.' It paused. '*Because* of you,' it added rather belligerently.

'No, I mean, put the light back on!'

Nothing happened.

Ellie was horrified. 'Now!'

There was no change, except for a quiet rustling in the darkness, as if the sprite had folded its arms in annoyance.

Ellie stamped her feet. 'Acorn, as Princess of Eidolon, I command you to turn your light back on right now!'

If anything, the cell got darker.

Ellie sat there, furious, for some minutes, waiting – but there was no change in the unrelieved blackness.

'Please,' Ellie wheedled at last. She wasn't normally polite when she wanted something, but it didn't seem as if the sprite would react well to her usual tactic of throwing a tantrum. And she really, really didn't like the dark. 'Oh, *please*, Acorn, just a little light.'

Seconds later a faint greenish light pulsed out of the sprite, casting long, thin shadows across the floor.

'Thank you,' Ellie said stiffly.

'Your family are trouble,' Acorn said after a time. 'Your mother abandoned us. Your brother got captured and had to be rescued. Now you, too.'

Ellie frowned. 'But Ben did save your cousin Twig.'

'Only after your uncle stole him from Eidolon.'

That was entirely true, but even so . . . 'You can't hold that against me!' she cried. 'Ben and I call him Awful Uncle Aleister: we hate him, and what he did was terrible! Dad told the police and they arrested him, and now he's in prison!'

Acorn's eyes whirled and glowed as if he was digesting this indecipherable information. Then he said, 'Your cousin, the witch, Cynthia: her cat killed my brother.'

Ellie had never heard Cynthia called a witch before: but now that she thought about it, her cousin *was* rather witchy, with her spiky nose and her carrot hair and her mean green eyes. She felt ashamed of the time she had spent with her, making jewellery out of the strange bits of fur and skin and feathers Cynthia had told her were 'offcuts' from her father's import business, and then selling them at school. Because now she understood exactly where those 'offcuts' had come from.

'I'm sorry about your brother,' she said. 'That's dreadful. Cynthia's cat is an absolute monster.'

'Is evil spy,' Acorn agreed. 'Sneak around for the Dodman, watching, always watching. No one is safe when the Sphynx is around: if it doesn't eat you, it hides and listens and carries tales to its master. Dodman learns who is causing trouble, who is still loyal to the Queen. And then the goblins come with their nets and sticks, beat and kill. Nasty creatures, have no loyalty to anything but their stomachs.'

Ellie was shocked. When she'd thought about her mother being the Queen of a magical other world, this kind of brutality and terror had never crossed her mind at all.

'We must get out of here! I can't have Mum giving herself up to the Dodman to save me; she's got to stop all this!'

'What can she do?' the sprite said gloomily. 'She away too long. No one believes in her any more.'

'She will take Eidolon back from the Dodman!' Ellie said furiously. 'She *will* banish him to the Other World so that he's no more than pathetic Mr Dodds, failed petshop owner!'

Acorn's thin, wheezy laugh was not one of delight, but of disbelief. 'Everyone is afraid of the Dodman and his monsters. They have lost hope for future. Cannot believe Queen will ever save them.'

'But they *must* believe, or it will never stop: it'll just get worse and worse and the Dodman will be able to do anything he wants!'

'He already does.'

'Well, I'm not going to let him. We're going to escape from here, you and I. Old Dogbreath isn't going to use *me* as a hostage!' And with that, Ellie marched over to the bucket and grabbed Acorn up. At once his green light turned a wild pink that flared out across the cell.

'Put me down!'

But Ellie was having none of it. Using the sprite as a torch she examined every inch of the prison's walls, every chink between the massive stones, every bit of loose mortar, every crack and cranny and crevice. She was just working her way around to the last corner of the cell, when the sprite coughed and recoiled.

'*Woo!* What a stink!'

And just as he said this, Ellie smelt it too. It was hot and musky and very, very strong. She wrinkled her nose; and sneezed and sneezed and sneezed. The smell seemed to be coming from a narrow gap between the stonework at the top of the wall. Standing on the bed, Ellie peered into the crack, holding Acorn out in front of her to illuminate her search, her heart beating wildly. She had *known* there was something hiding in the dark: she could sense it lurking, breathing, waiting . . .

At first she could see nothing; then something on the other side of the crack gleamed. She squinted, but her sight was poor at the best of times in Eidolon. She moved closer so that her nose was almost in the hole. The pink light from the woodsprite flooded the dark space. And then the thing that was gleaming *blinked.*

It was a very large, very dark eye.

Ellie shrieked.

On the other side of the wall there came the sound of a profound sigh. Then she heard, 'What did I do? All I did was blink.

I didn't roar, I didn't paw the ground, I didn't chase. I just blinked. Just a little twitch of the eye and already she's screaming. Women: I'll never understand them.'

Whatever it was, it sounded pretty miserable. Curiosity overcoming fear, Ellie applied her eye and the sprite to the hole again. 'Hello,' she said bravely, for there was a thick wall between her and the speaker. 'Who are you?'

In the darkness beyond there was a heavy silence, as if the occupant of the next cell was thinking very hard indeed. Then a deep voice rumbled out. 'Well, I could tell you I was a handsome hero, locked away by the Dodman and left to rot, but what would be the point in lying? You're in there and I'm in here and even if you want to run away from me you can't.' It took a deep breath. 'I'm the minotaur,' it admitted.

Ellie frowned. The name rang a distant bell in her head but she couldn't quite remember why. Something about an evil king who sent girls and boys into a labyrinth which they couldn't find their way out of, and something awful that lived at the heart of the maze . . . What sort of awful thing was it, though? What had made it so terrible? She gave up.

'Oh,' she said. 'Well, hello, Minotaur. My name's Ellie, and my mother's the Queen of Eidolon.'

'You're a *princess*?' The minotaur sounded disbelieving. 'Well, if you say so. I am, myself, a prince, of sorts, if not of such elevated status as yourself. Princess of Eidolon, indeed.' It snorted.

It was a huge snort, the sort of snort a bull might make. A really big bull.

Acorn shielded her from the worst of the blast, which was just as well. '*Eeeeewwww!* Get it off me, get it off!'

Ellie stared at the wood-sprite in disgust. It had already been pretty ugly to start with, unless you had a thing for twiggy creatures with raspberry eyes. But now it was covered from its head to its long, thin toes with thick green snot.

'Ugh!'

Ellie dropped the sprite without another second's thought, and wiped her hands instinctively down her jeans. Acorn gave her a furious look, then picked himself stickily up off the floor, walked disjointedly over to the bucket, scrambled up it and nose-dived into the stagnant water inside to take a long and noisy bath.

'Sorry,' said the voice on the other side of the wall. 'I must be allergic to something.'

Ellie made a face. Pathetic. *However*, she thought to herself, *whatever a minotaur is, if it's in these cells it must be the Dodman's enemy, and so by definition it must be my friend. However scary, or snotty, it may be.* She braced herself.

'So, why are you in here?' she asked boldly.

'The Dodman tried to make me work for him. But I bow to no man, and especially not to one with the head of a mangy hound.' He paused. 'Besides, he does not know my true name, and so cannot compel me. He captured me when I was being rather less vigilant than I should have been and tried to persuade me to his cause. He used the dogs on me after I killed a dozen of his goblins. Ghost-dogs are frustratingly hard to harm. He will go after the dinosaurs next. They may be more cooperative, being considerably more stupid than me.'

'What did he want you to do?'

'Why, to fight for him, to destroy the creatures who would take the Queen's side.'

'Are you very big and scary, then?' Ellie asked with a gulp.

'You could say that. Many are scared of me.' There was a pause. 'Though really there's little need. The stories about me are much worse than the truth.'

'Stories?' Now she was interested. 'What sort of stories?'

'If you haven't heard them, why should I tell you?'

There came a cackle from her own cell. 'Are you all so ignorant in the Other World?'

Ellie whirled around. All of the sprite's sharp little teeth were showing in a not-very-friendly grin. He was laughing at her. She gave him a hard stare. 'Why on earth should I know what it is?'

'Here, he is very famous,' Acorn said. 'A legend in his own lifetime.'

Despite herself, Ellie was impressed. 'Famous for what?'

'Eating folk.' The sprite's little eyes were bright with malice. 'Especially youngsters.'

Ellie felt a chill run down her spine. 'Do you?' she asked the chink between the stones, trying to keep the shake out of her voice.

'I'm not particularly proud of the fact,' the creature in the other cell replied quietly. 'And I wouldn't say I liked it much. Really I prefer a good patch of grass. Or some hay. Daisies, too. And meadowbells.'

Ellie didn't know what meadowbells were, but – daisies? She frowned. 'What are you, a cow or something?' Though she couldn't quite imagine a cow eating anyone.

'*Hmmph!*' The minotaur snorted in affront and the sound thrummed through Ellie's bones. 'A cow indeed!' He paused. 'What is a cow, anyway?'

'Even babies in our world know what cows are,' Ellie said contemptuously. 'They're big four-legged animals which stand around in fields, and chew grass and make milk and stuff.'

The minotaur was none the wiser, so he said nothing. Curious now, Ellie looked through the crack again, but this time all she could see was the merest slick of light from the shiny surface of a huge eyeball.

'I only have two legs,' he said after a while. 'You, on the other hands, from what I can see, don't look much like a Princess of Eidolon. Apart from anything else, your eyes aren't green.'

'I can't help that!' Ellie said crossly. 'I'm the oldest of the three of us; Ben's got one green eye and one brown; but Baby Alice has the same green eyes as Mum.'

On the other side of the wall there was a pause. Then the minotaur said, 'Three of you. That's interesting. And, may I ask, were you born in Eidolon?'

'Of course not! I was born in Bixbury General Hospital.'

'I have not heard of this place.'

'Bixbury, in Oxfordshire, England.'

A puzzled silence.

Ellie rolled her eyes. 'The United Kingdom, Europe. Planet Earth.'

'The Other World?'

Ellie thought about this. 'I suppose so,' she said dubiously.

From the other cell there came a great sigh. 'Three children from two worlds! Perhaps you are the children of the prophecy.'

'I don't know about any prophecy,' said Ellie.

'It's known only to the older ones of Eidolon, and no one has ever really given it much credence. Really, it's more of a nonsense poem, a nursery rhyme told to babes in arms.'

'Well, what is it then?' Ellie asked impatiently. 'I think if I'm in it I have a right to know.'

The minotaur took a deep breath:

'*One plus one is two*
And those two shall make three
Three children from two worlds
Will keep Eidolon free—'

On the other side of the wall, Ellie made a face. 'It's a bit vague, isn't it? It could mean anything.'

'If you hadn't interrupted me, I'd have told you the rest of it.'

'Oh. Well, I hope it's better than what you've already told me.'

'Do you know something?' the minotaur said. 'You're really very annoying. I'm beginning to wish I hadn't given up eating people after all. In fact, I might just take it up again. Once I'm out of here.'

Ellie bit her lip. 'Sorry. Do tell me the rest.'

'The last of it goes:

"*Three children from two worlds*

140

Three to save the day
One with beauty's spell to tame
One bravely to bring flame
And one with the power to name."'

Now Ellie's eyebrows shot up. '"Beauty's spell to tame." I rather like the sound of that,' she said softly.

'I don't think you'll be saving anyone,' came the sprite's scratchy voice. 'Stuck in here.' It paused. 'Anyway, you're not very beautiful.'

'What would an ugly little thing like you know about beauty?' Ellie said sharply. 'I read all the best magazines, you know. *Clobber* and *Warpaint* and *Hi!* There's not a beauty tip in the world I don't know. How to spend three hours achieving the "Natural Look". How to make your skin go orange without any smudges. How to stuff chicken fillets in your bra for a better cleavage—'

The sprite looked at her even more dubiously. 'Chicken fillets?'

Ellie waved her hands at it. 'Oh, I can't be bothered to try to explain to such an . . . ignoramus!' She thought for a moment; then her eyes gleamed. 'But I have a plan. And you, Acorn, are going to be the one who carries it out!'

CHAPTER SIXTEEN

The Book of Naming

'Speckle Greywing! Lily Spearwater! Gossamer Moonhorse!'

The Queen's voice rose high as a songbird's and Baby Alice clapped her hands in glee. 'Gossma!' she declared happily. 'Gossma, Gossma Moohoss!'

Moments later, three streaks of light burst out of the pale clouds above, circled once, twice, then plummeted towards the clearing like falling stars, resolving at last into three exhausted and not-very-happy-looking fairies.

'Why have you summoned us?' asked Speckle Greywing, his curls of blond hair in disarray, his pale cloak tattered as if from a sudden flight through brambles, or from the clutches of some taloned predator. He gazed around in amazement at the crowd already assembled there – the sylphs and the nymphs, the dryads and the gnomes, the sprites and elves, the centaurs and cats. They were thronged around every tree, seated upon each fallen log and hummock of turf; while mermaids and selkies jostled for space in the confined waters of the woodland stream.

'Yes, who do you think you are to drag us away without warning or request?' This came from the second of the fairies, tall and thin, her bony features set in a feral snarl.

'Oh do stop moaning, Gossamer,' said the third fairy. 'See, it is Cernunnos himself who has called us.'

'You need to clean out your ears, Lily: you must have got bees' nests in them!' Speckle declared furiously. 'It was a woman's voice I heard.'

'Bees don't make nests, stupid—' Lily Spearwater started.

The Lord of the Wildwood set down the Book of Naming he had been holding out for Isadora, put his hands on his hips and yelled. 'Be quiet, all three of you, and do obeisance to your Queen!'

'Queen? We have no Queen!' cried Speckle.

'Not since the last one deserted us,' sneered Gossamer.

'Oh!' cried Lily Spearwater as her violet gaze settled at last on the small blonde woman sitting on the log in the midst of the gathering, with a green-eyed baby in her lap. 'Oh my! Oh my goodness, it is . . . it is Isadora of Corbenic, though –' her voice dropped to a whisper and she spoke behind her hand '– she looks so old and tired . . .'

'There is no Corbenic any more,' Speckle said dismissively. 'It's Dodman Castle now, and I can't see that changing any time soon.'

Isadora firmed her jaw. 'It shall change,' she said, and her voice rang out across the clearing. 'It must. I will not see my country ruined by the Dodman and his ilk. But if it is to change, I will need your help: your help and the help of all the good folk of Eidolon.'

Speckle folded his arms. 'Why should we help you? You did not stay here to help us.'

'Show some respect for your Queen!' the Lord of the Wildwood roared, advancing upon the belligerent fairy, who soared quickly out of his way and took roost upon the branch of a willow which wept over the water's edge.

'Cernunnos,' Isadora said quietly, 'what Speckle Greywing says is quite fair, and he has the right to an explanation, as do all my subjects who have answered my call.' She looked up into the willow, where the two other fairies had joined Speckle. Then she looked around the clearing and raised her voice so that all might hear her words. 'When I left Eidolon, I did not know that my absence would result in this cruelty and wickedness. I did not know that my folk would suffer as they have. I did not know that the Dodman would grow so powerful by diminishing the magic in my world.' She hung her head. 'I really did not know very much at all. I am sorry for my ignorance and I know how all of you have suffered. All I can say in my defence is that I left Eidolon for love, which is the best reason in any world.'

At this, Baby Alice gurgled and cooed. 'Mama, Daddy!' she

said. 'Ben, Ellie, Alice!' Alice's eyes now blazed an unearthly green. 'The three!' she declared. 'Save Eidolon.'

Cernunnos's face went slack with astonishment, but after a few moments he recovered himself and said into the awed silence: 'It may have seemed to many of us that Isadora left our world for so long that the magic of the Secret Country and its folk were left dangling over an abyss by the thinnest of threads, but while she was lost to us she brought three children into the Other World.'

There was a murmur at this, then one of the dryads leant out of her tree and asked, '*The* three? Do you mean the children of the prophecy?'

The murmurs grew in volume now as the older ones gathered there explained the meaning of this to those who had no idea what was being talked about, until Cernunnos waved his arms and called for quiet.

'It may be that they are indeed the children of the prophecy, the three who will weave the magic back into Eidolon and drive the Dodman and his kind back into the shadows whence they came. The three who will be our salvation.' He dropped his eyes to Alice. 'Of course,' he added, 'it may also be that it will take some time to win back our world from the clutches of those who are trying to destroy it, for as you can see, Alice is very young indeed: too young yet to play any active part in the resistance against the Dodman.'

At this, Baby Alice turned her luminous gaze upon the Horned Man. 'Queen,' she said, quite distinctly. 'Me. Queen Alice.' She reached out her chubby little hands and waved them in a wide, inclusive gesture which took in all the gathered souls. 'Mine,' she said.

Cernunnos laughed, rather nervously. 'Well, Alice,' he said, 'we shall see about that in due course, I am sure.'

'Now, now, dear,' Mrs Arnold said softly to her daughter, 'let's not run before we can walk, hey?'

'Hay is for horses,' said a white cat, one of a group of nine who were sitting by her feet.

The Queen laughed and reached down to her and stroked her head, and the white cat leant her cheek into Isadora's palm. 'Indeed it is, Jacaranda; and for hippogriffs and minotaurs too, in a well-ordered world; and I hope Eidolon will be well-ordered again soon, with your aid and the aid of all those gathered here.'

'You will need more than a foolish old prophecy and a handful of fairies and tree-spirits and lesser beasts if you're to take on the Dodman and the monsters who will come to his call!' cried Speckle Greywing.

'Who are you calling a lesser beast, young man?' Jacaranda bristled fiercely, showing her hackles.

'Well, I can't quite see you taking on a tyrannosaurus rex or a dragon, can you?' Speckle sneered. 'One would rip your pretty white coat into shreds and the other would roast your skinny carcass and gobble you whole!'

'That's unkind,' the Queen said sharply. 'And I think you are doing Jacaranda a disservice: it is not always might which prevails in battle, but wit and courage, which the cats of Eidolon have in plenty.'

'Even so,' said Speckle, 'you will need the greater beasts to join your cause if you are to challenge the Dodman, and I do not even see a single dragon here.'

'Very true,' said one of the female centaurs, pawing the ground with a neat hoof. 'But that is because the Queen has not yet summoned them.'

One of the gnomes shouted, 'And then there's the trolls and the ogres too!'

His companion elbowed him in the ribs. She looked exactly like him – leathery skin, long white hair, twinkly blue eyes and hooked nose – except that she had no beard. 'Do pipe down, Grot!' She stepped out of the ring of gnomes and addressed the Queen boldly. 'It's good to see the bravery and loyalty of the woodland folk,' she said, acknowledging the crowd with a wave of her gnarled hand, 'but I agree that we will not stand long against the Dodman without allies from farther afield. We may not want the help of such as the trolls and ogres, for they were ever undependable and dark of heart, but I do not think we will fare well without at least the support of the fire-drakes.'

Cernunnos stepped before the Queen and bowed his head. 'Perhaps now is the time to summon the chieftains of the dragon clans,' he said, 'if we are to strengthen the will of your people.'

'Perhaps,' sighed Isadora.

'Though it must be said,' the Lord of the Wildwood added quietly, 'that dragons are volatile and arrogant beasts and can be very difficult to handle, let alone control in a limited space. Are you sure you will not change your mind and compel them as you summon them?'

The Queen looked around the clearing at the small creatures gathered there, her green eyes full of anxiety. Then she shook her head.

'No,' she said. 'Their choice must be a free one.'

She sat Baby Alice on the ground at her feet, picked up the Book of Naming and turned its pages to the one which bore the legend 'Dragons' . . .

CHAPTER SEVENTEEN

Terror

A great silver moon rose over the battlements of Dodman Castle, casting long thin shadows across the stonework like fingers of darkness. A tall figure stood silhouetted against the pale disc up on those battlements. It flung its head back and an unearthly howl ripped through the falling night; and all who heard it felt a sudden chill shiver through their bones.

As if awoken by the cry, a flock of bats came tumbling out of the crannies in the castle's wall and fled out across the lake in a clatter of wings. Somewhere in the woods beyond the lake's shore an owl hooted and was answered by the call of something Ben could not identify, but which made his skin creep and crawl as if a parade of ants had got under his clothes and were marching up and down his arms and legs.

'I must have miscalculated. We are too late!' Darius cried, gazing up at the castle in horror.

'What do you mean, "too late"?' said Ben.

'We need to save her before the moon is full . . .'

Ben frowned. 'Why? I mean, I know we need to rescue Ellie as fast as possible, but why by full moon?'

The centaur said nothing. He lifted his head and gazed up into the sky. A moment later, a veiling cloud slipped softly sideways and as it did so Darius gasped. 'Thank the heavens, it is not quite full, but it will surely be so before too long. We do not have much time.'

Iggy burrowed his head under Ben's arm. 'I hate this place,' he growled fervently. 'Please don't make me swim that lake again.'

This all came out as something of a mumble, but Ben hugged him anyway. 'We have to find Ellie,' he reminded the little cat.

'If he lays a claw upon her –' Darius turned his head to look at the boy on his back '– I swear I will break every bone in his loathsome body. I will stamp him underhoof. I will trample him till there is nothing left of him but bloody rags.'

Ben had never heard the centaur so fierce. Darius's eyes flared briefly silver in the moonlight and all at once he looked nothing at all like the friendly companion with whom Ben had shared so much of his time in Eidolon, but more like a savage creature from another world.

'I didn't know you liked her so much,' Ben said. 'You've only just met her.'

His hands, knotted in the coarse black mane, felt the sudden heat rising from the centaur's neck, and he realised with a start that Darius was blushing.

'But she is the Princess,' the centaur started. 'She is a Princess of Eidolon, daughter to Queen Isadora. I am pledged to her cause and I cannot fail her. I must not!' He paused. 'But she is also very beautiful.'

Ben laughed. 'Gosh,' he said, 'you must have terrible eyesight!'

From under his arm there came a great purr of delight. 'Who'd have thought it?' rasped Iggy in his best gravelly tones. 'A centaur falling in love with a human girl?'

'I am not "in love",' Darius said stiffly. 'And anyway, she is not a mere human. Be careful what you say, cat, or you will be swimming the lake sooner than you think.' He let that thought hang in the darkening air, then added, 'Besides, we cannot allow the Queen to give herself up to the Dodman.'

'What?'

Darius groaned. 'I am an idiot. Cernunnos would have my hide for such indiscretion.'

'Darius, I don't know what you're talking about. What do you mean about Mum giving herself up to the Dodman?'

Iggy squirmed free of Ben's embrace and ran up the centaur's neck. There, he dug his claws in and growled, 'Is the Queen in danger as well? You'd better tell us, now!'

Darius winced. Then he sighed and hung his head. 'You

have a right to know. A fairy – Nettle Blueflower – carried a message from the Dodman to the Lord of the Wildwood. He said that unless the Queen submitted herself to him before the moon was full, he would harm Eleanor. He said he would send her back piece by piece . . .'

Ben felt those last words echoing around his skull. Piece by piece. He imagined what the Dodman meant by that, and felt abruptly sick. It was horrible. He knew that his mother would never allow such a thing to happen. He swallowed as another thought occurred to him. 'But we could never trust the Dodman to let Ellie go, even if Mum did go to him!' he cried.

'I know.' Darius nodded. 'And that is why Cernunnos thought it best she did not know what was in the message.'

'Then she doesn't even know that the Dodman holds Ellie prisoner?'

Darius shook his head.

'Dad will tell her!' Ben said fiercely.

'Your father is asleep. He will not wake up until he leaves the Lord of the Wildwood's realm.'

Ben stared at him. He understood why the Lord of the Wildwood had done what he had done, but even so it seemed to him wrong in a way he could not fully explain. He felt tears prick his eyes.

'So it's down to us to save Ellie, then,' he said grimly.

'Take heart, Ben,' rasped Iggy. 'We will save your sister.' He paused. 'Though I do wish it didn't mean having to swim the horrid lake again.'

*

The Dodman stared out over the moonlit lake. 'Where is she?' he hissed, scanning the dark shore on the other side. He whistled and clicked his fingers and a great bird cast itself gracefully from the top of the tallest of the castle's towers, wheeled lazily downwards around the spire and came to rest on the crenellations a little distance away, where it folded its leathery wings and regarded its master with its head on one side. Moonlight played off one beady eye and down the length of its long, long bill.

'Boggart, a snack!' the Dodman demanded, and one of the goblins detached itself from the group lurking in the shadows and stepped forward, patting its pockets thoughtfully.

After a moment it pulled out a sack, and from that drew a small, striped catlike creature, which hissed and growled and showed its sabre teeth.

The Dodman shook his head irritably. 'We are not here for sport, Boggart! Let the beast go and give Terror something more suitable.'

Looking puzzled, Boggart dropped the sabre-toothed tiger cub on the ground and everyone backed away at speed. It ran around in furious little circles before eventually fastening its jaws in one of Grizelda's ankles and giving her a very nasty nip. Apparently not liking how the giantess tasted, it recoiled, spitting. Then it fled through the tower's door and down the stone steps. A few moments later there was a dreadful hubbub in the courtyard below followed by the yelp of a ghost-dog in pain.

The Dodman rolled his great black eyes. Then he cuffed

Boggart soundly around the head. 'A perfectly ordinary vampire chicken was all that was needed, idiot!' He turned on his heel. 'Bogie!'

A second goblin came forward eagerly, flourishing a small feathered creature with wicked red eyes and a pair of sharp teeth protruding from the corners of its beak. The Dodman took it from Bogie's claws and tossed it to the thing on the battlement, which snatched it out of the air and swallowed it down in a single great gulp. You could track the course of the snack by the bulge which travelled, fighting all the way, down that long, leathery throat into the monster's gullet.

'You will overfly the forest,' the Dodman instructed it, once it had wiped its beak once or twice against its featherless hide, 'and look for the Queen. See if you can mark her progress towards the castle. Then return here to me and tell me what you have seen. Go now.'

'Yes, master!' the creature croaked and, gathering its haunches, leapt off into the night.

The Dodman watched it go with some satisfaction.

'Well, let us hope that Isadora is doing the right thing,' he declared. 'Or it may have to be that a little part of her precious daughter will be leaving here soon without the rest.'

The goblins all sniggered delightedly at that and started taking bets on which bit of Ellie their master might send with his message.

'Surely a heron should not be flying around in the dead of night?' growled Iggy.

Ben shut his left eye and stared upwards with his Eidolon eye. He gasped, blinked; stared again. He remembered the pictures in the book he had been reading before he left the Other World. 'That's not a heron!' he cried. 'It's a pterodactyl!'

Darius shaded his eyes and watched the dark shape planing through the night sky. 'Ah,' he said softly. 'Yes, that is Terror. One of the Dodman's favourite spies. An ancient creature, cruel and wicked. We had better withdraw beneath the shelter of the trees till it is gone.'

So saying, he backed quickly away into the eaves of the forest. From the safety of the darkness there they watched the prehistoric bird glide above them, the moonlight silvering its wide wings and glinting eyes, and Ben felt a shiver run down his spine.

A few moments later it flew directly overhead, and Ben held his breath, sensing its cold gaze on the back of his neck. But without hesitation it carried on in the direction from which they had travelled that day, towards the Wildwood. Through the canopy of branches Ben glimpsed it looking this way and that as it progressed, sometimes circling as if something had caught its attention.

'Cernunnos has his own lookouts posted throughout the Wildwood,' Darius said quietly, as if reading Ben's thoughts. 'The owls and wood-sprites will alert him to Terror's presence. Do not worry: he will keep your family out of sight. There is nothing more useful that we can do than continue with our task.'

And so, they emerged on to the dewy grass leading down to the shore of the wide lake once again, and there Ben dismounted and set the little cat down on the pebbles at his feet, where Iggy at once set to dealing with his ruffled fur. Which was infinitely preferable to thinking about what might have to happen next.

CHAPTER EIGHTEEN

The Dragons

'Sheherazade! Masaranshak!'

It was many long years since Isadora had had any dealings with the fire-drakes of her world, and then she had been little more than a child, and they had been figures out of legend, rarely glimpsed in her corner of Eidolon – at least around the tamer environs surrounding Corbenic Castle. Dragons were beasts about whom the great stories were woven; stories about treasure and treachery, about battles and broken vows, heroes and burning halls, fire and fear. She had never seen dragons any closer than the pair she had witnessed from her bedroom window, chasing one another, skimming their wingtips across the surface of the lake in the summer of the year in which she turned seventeen. For twenty minutes she had watched them in their mating game, and had thought them magnificent, noble creatures; a wondrous sight with the sun burnishing their coloured scales and gilding the wisps of smoke which escaped their wide nostrils as they dived and soared. It was hard to equate such grace with the tales of murderous mayhem her old nurse had cheerfully regaled her with late at night, tales designed to chasten a child who would not go to sleep when told to. Even then, the stories had made the young Isadora's eyes sparkle with excitement and filled her dreams with glorious images and the thrill of flight.

She shivered as, with all those present, she surveyed the night sky in anticipation mixed with dread.

Two dark shapes fled across the face of the moon, and still she held her breath. They circled lazily, then stooped like a pair of falcons diving upon prey. Air displaced from the great beats of their wings stirred the foliage around them like a wind; and then the first dragons she had ever summoned descended into the clearing.

Queen Isadora held her breath.

In a burst of jewelled colour, the dragons landed.

'Who is it who has the temerity to summon us?' roared the first, and a thin sheet of fire accompanied his words, lighting up the dark air.

Isadora's eyes flashed. Above her head, the dried winter leaves of an oak smoked and crisped. Two burst into flame and spiralled down from the tree like falling fireflies. She stepped forward. 'I have done so,' she said bravely, gazing at this fero-cious apparition. 'I am Isadora, Queen of Eidolon, and I have called you here to ask you for your help.'

The second dragon came up beside her mate and cocked her head on one side, regarding the Queen, unblinking. A long, thin black pupil split the gold of the iris, like a cat's eye in sun-light. At last she said, 'Help? What "help" is it that you need that you must summon dragons?'

'The Dodman threatens the very existence of Eidolon. He seeks to destroy its magic, and he is gathering his forces in order to do so. We must defeat him and drive him from our world. But we cannot do it alone, we cannot defeat him without the fire-drakes.'

'Why should we care about the idiot dreams of the Dodman? He is but a puny little wingless man with the head of a jackal: he poses no threat to us.'

'He is cunning and cruel, and his ambitions know no bounds. He has been destroying the small creatures, one by one. He has taken them from our world, and with each one that fails, magic is lost. Without magic, no dragons will fly in the skies of Eidolon.'

The larger of the two dragons, his scales a brilliant emerald-green, raised his head. Two wisps of smoke ghosted from his nostrils. 'The Dodman is no threat to us,' he declared haughtily. 'We are too mighty for him. Or for you. Come, Sheherezade, let us leave these fools to their games.'

The female dragon, Sheherezade, said, 'I have heard some of this talk before, but it seemed like nonsense then, as it does now. And I do not take kindly to being called across half of Eidolon to answer the summons of some elf-woman who is no queen of mine, nor, for her long absence, of any others in this world.'

Isadora went pale. Cernunnos put a hand on her arm. 'Steady, my lady . . .' he started, but two spots of hectic colour had appeared in the Queen's cheeks.

'We are all of Eidolon,' she said softly, but there was an edge to her voice. 'And we all share responsibility for our world. I have been away, but now I am back, and I am Queen, and I swear I will stop the Dodman, whatever it may take.'

Masaranshak coiled and uncoiled his long, scaly tail like an irritated cat making up its mind whether to bite someone. 'Well, you must do so without our aid,' he said. 'Your quarrel is not ours. The Roix Clan have had no trouble from the one you call the Dodman, and we have better things to do than interfere in the petty squabbles of the unwinged.'

'Halt!'

The voice came from above them, and everyone looked up. A great dark shape was looming closer, the moonlight gleaming off its scales, which gleamed in wonderful shades of crimson and gold.

'Do not challenge me, Xarkanadûshak!' Masaranshak bellowed, and a long spiny ridge running the length of his long neck rose just like the hackles of an angry dog.

Zark stared at the clan-chief and his purple eyes whirled and whirled. 'I am not here to challenge you, Maz,' he said grimly, 'but to warn you. The Dodman has his spy out, the vile pterodactyl, Terror. He is searching for the Queen. If he takes her, his power will be immeasurable. Ishtar is keeping him away for now, but others will come. The Queen needs our help: would you be so cowardly as to deny her?'

The spines jutted dangerously, and little sparks of fire shot out of Masaranshak's nostrils. 'Just who are you calling a coward, Zark?'

'Yes,' hissed Sheherazade, 'you can hardly speak of cowardice, you who were too weak to stop the dog-headed one taking you captive! You bring shame upon our whole race.'

'Now, now, Sherry,' Maz began, and his spines lowered a few degrees. 'Zark did go back into the Other World to rescue the others who were taken—'

'Weaklings, all, to allow the Dodman to trap them so! They do not deserve the name of fire-drake; they are no better than worms!'

From the skies above the Wildwood there came a harsh shriek. Then the darkness was split apart by a sheet of flame.

Zark's head shot up anxiously, but in the aftermath of the fire-blast there was nothing to be seen, and a cloud had drifted across the moon. He dragged his eyes away from where his wife and the pterodactyl did battle above them.

'In ancient days we were one clan,' he reminded Masaranshak. 'Shall we not be so again, to the glory of our kind, united in the name of Eidolon?'

Sheherazade ruffled her wings impatiently. 'No, we shall not. The Roix Clan have fought hard these long years for their territory and their rights, and we shall not be parting with either easily – especially to dragons of lesser heritage and abilities. Come, Maz,' she declared imperiously. 'I'm not staying here to listen to wheedlers and whiners.'

And with that she bunched her mighty haunches and leapt skywards, to be followed a moment later by her mate.

Isadora watched them go in dismay. Cernunnos put a hand on her shoulder.

'They are but two among a dozen dragon clan-chiefs,' Zark said gently. 'Not all may be as arrogant as these.' He turned away so that none might see the doubt in his eyes. 'At least, I hope not,' he whispered into the dark air.

CHAPTER NINETEEN
Old Friends

On the shores of the lake which stretched to the jagged outlines of the Dodman's stronghold, Queen Isadora's son had his own summons to make.

'She Who Swims the Silver Path of the Moon!'

Ben tried to call as quietly as he could, for fear that the Gabriel Hounds might hear him and give them away by baying their heads off. Then he thought: actually, if they do bay their heads off, that would be a jolly good thing! He imagined them all running blindly around, bumping into each other and treading on each others' snapping jaws, yelping when they got bitten by the fallen heads. He was so taken up by this gruesome image that he didn't even notice when a pale shape broke the waters of the lake, followed by another, and another.

'Ben!'

It was barely more than a whisper, but it made Ben's heart skip a beat.

In the moonlight, it looked for a moment as if the sleek head of a seal had emerged from the waters of the lake; then, as the magical air of Eidolon touched it, the long, full muzzle contracted and gave way to something much more human in appearance. Where moments before there had been great, sprouting whiskers there was smooth, white skin; where there had been huge black, glistening eyes, now there were eyes of a pale and gentle grey; and where there had been a mottled sheen, there was a flow of pale hair which cascaded from the top of the speaker's head to pool upon the surface of the water.

'Silver!'

And there she was: Silver the selkie, the girl who was neither truly girl nor seal, but a tantalising combination of both.

Ben could not help but grin from ear to ear. Despite the desperate situation they faced, he felt unaccountably happy, as if his heart had somehow grown too big for his ribs.

'Oh, Silver, you came!'

'How could I not? You summoned me. But, Ben, it is so good to see you.' Her gaze rested on him gravely, then her wide grin matched his own and suddenly she was laughing, and it was like the sound of a mountain stream trickling down rocks. With a powerful flick of her body, she propelled herself up on to the shore, where the moonlight blurred the way the flippers changed to limbs and the sheen of wet skin gave way to the soft folds of a thin white dress.

A moment later, she had hugged him so hard that he could hardly breathe. Even though she was now much more girl than seal, he could still feel the cold of her body seeping into him as if from the ocean depths. When she kissed him on the cheek, he could have sworn he felt the ghost of her whiskers against his chin.

At last she broke away from him, and surveyed the other two members of Ben's expedition.

She nodded first to the centaur, then to Iggy. 'Hello, Master Wanderer,' she said, and the little black-and-brown cat yowled delightedly.

Behind Silver, two figures were making their way into the shallows. The first was Melusine.

'Mellie!' Ben cried delightedly, and was about to step forward until he remembered the mermaid's last words to him, about taking him down to her lair, to eat him. 'How . . . er . . . nice to see you again,' he finished lamely, keeping well out of range.

Beyond Mellie, the third figure was imposing: at first glance as big as an elephant seal, or a walrus. But when Ben turned his Eidolon eye upon it, he could see that the top half, at least, was man: a great, tall, bare-chested man with a wild mop of curly blond hair and eyes which, even by moonlight, were the colour of a summer sky. And those eyes were assessing him very carefully, as if weighing him up and taking stock of what he saw.

'Hello, Ben Arnold,' he boomed. 'My name is He Who

167

Hangs Around on the Great South Rock to Attract Females –
but you can call me sir.'

Ben stared at him, not sure what to say to this.

The selkie burst into a great gust of laughter, which
sounded like the crash of surf against a reef. 'Call me Skerry,' he
said at last. 'I am Silver's father.'

Ben smiled uncertainly. 'It's nice to meet you, Mr Skerry,
sir.' Remembering his manners, he started to extend an arm to
shake hands with the selkie; then he saw the moonlight glinting
off Mellie's sharp teeth close by – too close; thought better of it
and nodded respectfully instead.

'So, Benjamin,' Skerry continued, his big voice carrying
over the water like the roar of the wind over the ocean, 'why
have you brought us here? We were diving in the Western Sea,
chasing some Greater Striped Catfish in and out of the rocks,
and we'd only eaten one or two. So it's really not very conven-
ient!' He inserted a finger into his mouth, and drew out a
shining white fishbone, which he threw over his shoulder.

Iggy shuddered. 'My poor cousins,' he said, then winked at
Ben.

'Oh, Dad,' Silver said crossly, 'stop giving my friend a hard
time. You know perfectly well it was me who asked you to come
along. And I'm quite sure that if Ben's used a summons it must
be for a very good reason. Although,' she added, turning her
candid grey gaze on Ben, a tinge of pink blooming in her
cheeks, 'it's always nice to see him.'

'It *is* for a good reason,' Ben insisted, feeling his own blush
rising. 'It's because the Dodman has got my sister Ellie.'

'Oh!' Silver's hand rose to her mouth. 'Oh, Ben, that's terrible.'

'It gets worse,' Iggy growled. 'Unless we can rescue her by full moon the Dodman is going to hurt her. He's using her as a hostage to make the Queen give herself up to him.'

'Mellie told us that Queen Isadora had come home,' Silver said softly. 'But we already knew, for the air felt clearer, the winter sun is warmer, the water smoother, and the catfish seemed livelier than they used to be—'

'Very good sport,' her father interjected. He regarded Ben, his blue gaze as keen as a hawk's. 'And he's holding the Princess in the castle?'

'We believe so,' Darius said.

'So you need us to carry you across the lake,' Skerry said matter-of-factly.

Ben nodded. 'Yes. I'm sorry to take you away from chasing the catfish.'

Skerry placed a huge hand on his shoulder. 'Do not apologise, young man. The catfish will wait until we've rescued your sister. Sometimes, though not often –' and one of his great blue eyes closed in a slow wink '– there are things which are more important than simple pleasure.' He paused. 'Do you know where they will have taken her?'

Ben shook his head. 'I doubt it will be where they kept me,' he said, 'since I managed to get out.'

'He will be taking no chances,' Darius agreed. 'There are dungeons, prison cells . . .'

Ben shuddered.

Skerry considered this. 'I imagine those would be down in the foundations of the castle,' he mused.

At this, Melusine snorted. 'That is indeed a long way down, my dear boy!'

Skerry regarded her warily. 'What do you mean?'

'There have been many fortresses where Corbenic now stands; fortresses lost to war and fire and flood, each built on the ruins of the last. I remember the old ways. In my youth – which is a very long time ago – the sealmen and I used to play nip-chase here.'

She sighed as if remembering happier days.

'Nip-chase?' Ben asked curiously.

The old mermaid bared her long, sharp teeth at him. 'If you caught one, you nipped him,' she cackled. 'Just a little nip, no more than a caress . . .'

Ben had sometimes played kiss-chase in the school playground; which mainly consisted of him running away from the older girls as fast as his legs could carry him, for they seemed to like him a lot more than he liked them. That had been bad enough, but at least it had been on dry ground and no one had been trying to bite him!

'I don't know why, but those selkies used to try to get away from me any way they could,' she sighed. 'In and out of those ancient ruins we swam, and they would dash up into the tunnels and grow their legs back just to escape me.'

Ben could quite understand why: if he'd been some poor selkie being chased by Mellie in her ravenous youth, he'd have been getting out of the water as fast as he could, too.

'And might those tunnels lead up to the current castle's dungeons?' the centaur asked.

Melusine shrugged. 'I don't know, but they must come out somewhere.'

'Then lead on, my beauty!' Skerry declared with his most flattering smile. 'The moon's not getting any thinner!'

'But, Dad—' Silver started, and her face was suddenly grave. 'What about . . .' and she leant in close to her father and whispered something to him.

Skerry grinned. 'Nautilus? Where would the Dodman get a nautilus from? They've been extinct even in the Southern Ocean for centuries.'

'Well, it's what I heard,' Silver said crossly, folding her arms. 'You never take anything I say seriously. And sometimes the mermen are right, you know.'

Ben couldn't help but grin: now the selkie sounded just like his sister. 'Wow,' he said. 'I'd love to see a nautilus!' He could imagine one now, just like in the adventure stories he loved so much – a giant squid with its tentacles wrapped around some hapless ship, dragging it down to the ocean bed to devour everyone aboard. Hmmm, perhaps he didn't want to see one close up after all.

He almost jumped a mile when something grabbed him; but it wasn't a giant squid, it was Skerry's massive arm. A moment later he had been deposited on the big selkie's wide back and they were off into the lake, following the flick of the mermaid's tail. Ben turned just in time to see Silver catch a firm hold of Iggy, and Darius wading into the water behind the pair of them, and then he found he had to hold on tight, since He Who Hangs Around on the Great South Rock to Attract Females had transformed rather rapidly from man to seal, and had become as slippery as a fish.

The last time Ben had crossed the lake, it had been with the Gabriel Hounds snapping at his heels – and worse. He remembered how they had gained on him and Silver, how he had thought all was lost, and the way his heart had risen at the sight of the Horned Man and the centaur on the shore, flanked by a pack of white wolves. And then he remembered how the wolves had leapt into the water to do battle with the hounds, but how the Dodman had somehow managed to harness the wolves so that their tails quivered between their legs, and how from then they did his bidding.

He shivered, expecting at any moment to hear the baying of the hounds, but their passage across the still waters of the lake was apparently going unnoticed. He was just about to relax and enjoy the strange sensation of travelling at speed on the back of the great selkie when a shriek split the air behind them, and when he turned to look back, he saw how a line of flame lit up the sky above the Wildwood.

Immediately, Skerry cried, 'Hold on, Ben!' and dived.

Ben just had time to take a deep breath and think, *Oh no*, because he did not much like getting his head underwater and had almost drowned in the local swimming pool when learning life-saving (which was pretty ironic), when the lake closed over him and he was engulfed in a world of murk and shadow.

He had closed his eyes instinctively as soon as Skerry had

dived, but now he opened his Eidolon eye cautiously and looked around. The selkie was barrelling through the water like a torpedo, twisting and turning through tall weeds and columns of stone; but Ben felt curiously safe down here, for Skerry was clearly in his element, and the pressure of the water seemed to hold him in place on the selkie's back. He almost forgot to hold his breath when they passed beneath a great decorated archway and into what seemed to be an elaborate courtyard, long abandoned and drowned by the subsequent invasion of the lake. Statues lay toppled here and there amongst the weeds and rubble: he could make out the broken image of a man with a pair of dragon's wings on his back, and the slim figure of a woman in a long dress standing on a plinth. As they passed this statue, Ben stared and stared: for the face was just like his mother's. He opened his mouth in shock; and the water rushed in.

CHAPTER TWENTY

Beneath the Castle

'Look at the state of you!'

The Dodman took in the tattered appearance of his spy with curiosity. The pterodactyl had flapped uncoordinatedly back to the castle and had barely managed to clear the battlements: he was clearly on his last wings. Or wing; for one was folded uselessly beneath him and was burned to an almost unrecognisable mess of charred bone and skin. The whole of one side of his leathery body was blackened, and he smelt even more appalling than usual. The dog-headed man wrinkled his muzzle in distaste.

'What happened to you? Did you fall in some troll's cook-fire?'

Terror regarded the Dodman with an unblinking, expressionless eye, which gave the impression that had he been uninjured he might have skewered the dog-headed man with his murderous beak.

'*Cark!*' he cried. 'Dragons. Over Wildwood. Four of them.'

He omitted to explain that he had received his wounds from a single dragon, and a female one at that.

The Dodman frowned. 'And the Queen?'

'No sign,' squawked the pterodactyl. 'But many creatures in Wildwood. Gathering.'

'What is she playing at?' the Dodman growled. 'Her daughter is in my dungeons under threat of death and she is throwing a party!'

Terror made a strangled noise, which might have been an expression of disgust, a laugh, or some other less obvious emotion. Then his legs gave way beneath him and he collapsed on to the stone floor, his breathing shallow and ragged.

The goblins, who until now had been keeping their distance, watched with interest. To them, the smell of barbecued pterodactyl wing was one of the most delicious things they could imagine in their wildest dreams (and goblins' dreams are wilder than most). Beetle stared at the felled creature with beady eyes; Batface was drooling openly. But it fell to Boggart, always the boldest of them, to put the question that each of them itched to ask: 'Master, when he's dead can we eat him?'

The Dodman's face was like thunder as he considered how

lightly the Queen was taking his threat. Time to send another, more graphic message. He turned sharply on his heel.

'Why wait till he's dead?' he said dismissively. What good was he with a broken wing? There were plenty more ptero-dactyls in the Shadow World to be captured and tamed and compelled to his will.

'And how is my little Princess?' the Dodman called through the cell door.

Inside, Ellie stiffened. She looked at the sprite. 'Ready?' she whispered.

Acorn blinked his raspberry-red eyes at her and gave a short nod.

'Actually,' she called, 'I feel dreadful!'

And as she said this, she realised abruptly that it was true. Her head felt as if someone had locked it in a vice and was tightening it, twist by twist. She swallowed. What if she was really ill? What if she died in here, in this horrid cell, in the dark, and no one knew? It was an awful thought.

There was a pause on the other side of the door. Then she heard the clanking sound and the grate of iron on iron as the key was inserted in the lock. Acorn launched himself from the edge of the bucket and hovered in the dark. Not even the faintest glow of pink emerged from him now and Ellie felt a sudden surge of admiration for the way he suppressed his fear.

As the Dodman opened the door and stared in, Ellie cried out, 'Oh my head!' and was promptly sick on the floor.

The Dodman stared at her with an expression of faint disgust.

'Your dear mother has not yet responded to our demands,' he told Ellie smoothly, watching her wipe her mouth on the sleeve of her T-shirt. His great black lips curved back in a wide grin which showed off his array of ivory dog's teeth. 'And the deadline is running out. The moon is almost full, but it seems that simple love for her daughter is not sufficient to bring her to me. I shall have to send her a more tangible message!'

Ellie was not quite sure what he meant by this; and at the moment she didn't entirely care.

'I really don't feel well,' she croaked. 'If I die, you won't be able to use me as a hostage.'

The Dodman laughed callously. 'She won't know that, though, will she? A dead girl's ear looks much the same as a live girl's ear, when it has been cut off.'

Ellie's hands instinctively clamped themselves over her ears, and so she did not hear Bogie whoop triumphantly at winning the bet he had taken with Brimstone and Bosko – which meant that he would get their share of Moloccan cockroaches tonight at dinner.

Ellie stared at Acorn. 'Go on!' she hissed. 'Go now! Quickly!'

The sprite stared at her with its complex ruby eyes, and for a long moment of doubt she thought he would stay and watch the sport. But as the goblins advanced, giggling, into the cell, his wings flexed and he launched himself from the lip of the bucket, over their heads and out into the corridor, unseen by the motley collection of creatures gathered there, all of whom were peering into the darkness of the cell with undisguised anticipation . . .

Acorn sped down the corridor, beating his wings with all the power that fear could lend him. He kept high up in the shadows beyond the lit sconces on the walls, in case any more goblins came wandering past. He hated goblins. He hated the Dodman, as he hated all the vile creatures in this castle. He was not an old wood-sprite, Acorn, and he had not known hatred for long in his life; but his faith in the world had been shaken by recent events and now it was hard to like or trust anyone. Which was why, now that he was free, he fully intended to stay free; to escape the castle as fast as he possibly could, return to the little copse where he had been captured, gather those friends and family he could find there and persuade them to fly with him far away from this terrible place, away from the influence of the dog-headed one and away from the Queen and her followers. He did not want to be caught up in the war that threatened, for he had already seen too much horror and had no wish to see more. So the little Princess would have to fare as best she could without him. He had carefully made Ellie no promise that he could be kept to; and once she was dead, no one would know he had not done the thing she had asked of him.

Apart from the minotaur.

He shook his head as he flew, as if to dispel that nagging

thought. The minotaur was never leaving the dungeons alive. And neither would he, if he did not find a way out soon.

He turned a corner which offered the prospect of stairs up, stairs down, and a long line of locked doors. A pair of goblins lounged on the stairs which led upwards, engrossed in a game which consisted of throwing a pair of bones up into the air and making bets on how they landed. It looked like the dullest game in the world; he could not imagine it would hold their interest very long. And so instead of flying past them, he took the passageway which led downwards into darkness.

'Ben. Ben! Wake up!'

Something wet and warm dripped on to his cheek. Was it raining? But rain wasn't usually warm. And surely it didn't rain underwater, which was the last place he could remember being. Then something rough rasped his skin. He opened his eyes, not knowing what to expect.

Two faces loomed over him. Two pairs of eyes peered at him intently – one pair of black pupils ringed with amber, the others huge and grey. Then the amber eyes came closer, and something wet and soft and smelling of water and fish pushed against his forehead. It made a vast rumbling sound, like the engine of a lorry.

A moment later another splash of warm liquid hit him squarely on the nose.

He pushed himself up awkwardly on to his elbows, blinking, and water ran out of his nose and mouth and hair.

'*Ugh!*'

'Oh, Ben, I thought you were dead!' Even with tears swimming in her eyes, Silver was grinning wildly.

'Yeah, you looked like a goner!' Iggy shook himself vigorously, sending a shower of lakewater over everyone in his proximity. 'Food for the fishes! Or –' and here he dropped his voice to a melodramatic whisper '– for the old mermaidy.' He cocked his head sideways.

Ben stared past Iggy's shoulder to where Melusine lay in a pool, watching him avidly. Beside her, Skerry was helping Darius up out of the water, hauling him by the arms. The centaur's hooves slipped and slithered on the weed-covered ruins, then he was up and out of the water, his long black hair plastered to his shoulders.

Ben looked around. They were in a sort of cave, except that it was no natural construction, being full of masonry and stonework and columns in all different styles. It was quite dark, apart from an array of tiny bright gold lights dotted around the 'cave' walls. Ben frowned. They looked like Christmas lights, the sort that people hung outside their houses to cheer up the neighbourhood in the depths of winter. But surely they didn't have Christmas in Eidolon?

He was about to get up and investigate when one of the lights detached itself and flew at him. He put his hands up in front of his face instinctively to ward it off, but it didn't hit him. Instead, when he peered around his fingers, he found himself looking at a tiny creature with a glowing head.

'Wow,' he said, impressed. How amazing to be able to light up your entire head. Imagine if people could do that: the Other

World would be a much more cheerful place. 'Hello.'

But the tiny thing zigzagged away at speed to rejoin its fellows.

'Fire-fairies,' Iggy explained matter-of-factly, licking the fur dry between his spread toes. 'A bit like fireflies in your world. Very shy.' He paused. 'Tasty, though, if you can catch 'em.' He looked at Ben enigmatically, his eyes as round as an owl's.

Ben stared back at him, horrified.

'Only joking,' Iggy rasped. 'Nearly had ya there.'

Tunnels led away out of the back of the cave-area; narrow and steeply stepped, leading away into pitch-darkness.

'Which one should we take?' Skerry asked.

A small voice in Ben's head went 'eeny meeny miny mo' and came up with the right-hand tunnel; but it was from the passage on the left-hand side that an ear-splitting shriek emerged.

High-pitched and full of pain, it echoed down the steep steps and out into the cavern where they stood. The fire-fairies shattered away from the walls as if an electric current had passed through them, and shot crazily about the chamber so that when Ben blinked, neon afterimages of their light-trails showed on the inside of his eyelids.

'Oh my,' breathed Silver. 'What was that?'

Ben shook his head fearfully. 'I don't know.' He didn't think it sounded like Ellie; but he could not really ever remember his sister shrieking in such a fashion, even when she had been dress-making for her dolls and had managed to stab her hand with some scissors. Even so, the hairs stood up on the back of his neck.

'Come on, Iggy,' he said. 'Cats see best in the dark. You'd better lead the way.'

Iggy looked at him doubtfully, stuck his head into the tunnel and promptly sneezed. 'Must I?'

'For Ellie,' Ben reminded him. 'And Eidolon.'

It is hard to see a cat's expression at the best of times, let alone in the dark of a cave, but Ben thought his friend looked both scared and resigned to the fact that he had to be their guide. In any case, Iggy squared his shoulders and stepped into the tunnel.

The air in the tunnel was chill and dank, pressing against skin and fur like fog. It smelt old and disused, as if nothing had breathed it in a hundred years. And it was very, very dark.

With a gulp, Ben took a step upwards, his hands spread out on either side of him. The walls felt wet and slippery, as if they were alive and giving off a cold sweat in a similar state of fear to his own.

Up he went, feeling his way. Behind him was Silver; then Darius, his hooves clattering on the stone; and finally Skerry. They reached the top of one flight and then the steps bent around a corner so that the little illumination given off by the fire-fairies was lost to them and they proceeded in total darkness.

Until a series of strange pink shadows suddenly danced on the walls ahead of them, and then something small and glowing shot over their heads and carried on rapidly down the stairs.

Ben stared after it. 'What was that?'

'I'll go and look,' Skerry's voice boomed back.

There came the sound of his feet pounding down the stairs . . . then nothing.

'Let's keep going,' said Ben. 'He'll catch us up in a minute.'

At the top of the stairs they emerged into a corridor which stretched to left and right of them. Closed doors lined both sides. Faint light showed at the far right-hand end.

'That way,' declared Ben grimly. 'Run on ahead, Iggy, and see what you can see.'

The cat squinted at him. 'I can tell you're royalty,' he said with a sniff. 'Giving orders an' all.' But he did as he had been asked, all the same.

He came back a moment later, looking nervous. 'Goblins,' he reported. 'Guards, I suppose, though they don't look very professional about it.'

Darius looked down at his hooves. 'Even so, I don't think there's much chance of me creeping past them,' he said dubiously.

Ben frowned. He hadn't thought about that. He was about to open his mouth to say as much when Skerry reappeared behind the centaur, clutching something triumphantly, something which lit the tunnel with an eerie glow. 'My practice at catching flying-fish came in handy,' Skerry grinned, brandishing his prize.

Ben felt himself grinning foolishly.

'Twig?' he asked, hardly daring to believe his eyes.

'He says his name is Acorn,' Skerry replied. 'But he won't say anything else.'

Indeed, the wood-sprite did not look at all happy with the

situation, as Ben could tell from the red light exuding between the fingers of Skerry's huge fist, and from the way its face was screwed up, and its arms were tightly folded.

'Hello, Acorn,' he said. 'Do you know a sprite called Twig?'

'My cousin,' Acorn replied shortly.

Ben nodded. 'Then you might have heard about me,' he continued. 'I found Twig in the Other World and helped him to get back here. My name is Ben, and I promise we're not going to hurt you.'

Acorn's beady eyes fixed upon him. 'Another one,' he said. 'I might have known.'

'Another one?'

'Your family bring trouble, every one of you.'

Ben scrutinised the wood-sprite coolly, trying not to get cross. 'Just how many of my family do you know—?' he started.

'Just the one, personally,' Acorn said. 'Eleanor, I think she said. Though now you have introduced yourself to me, I suppose I can claim two.' He stared at Ben defiantly, then added, 'All I want is to get out of here – which is just what I'd have done if the huge fishy lummox who's currently squeezing the life out of me hadn't caught me while I was trying to escape. It's not a lot to ask, really, is it, given all the trouble your family have brought our way?'

He closed his eyes as if pained. It seemed his plan of leaving this place quickly and quietly was bound to failure.

'Where is she?' Ben asked grimly.

The wood-sprite sighed and hung his head. At last he whispered, 'You're too late, you know.'

Ben remembered the terrible cry they had heard and his heart skipped a beat, then thundered against his ribs. 'Too late?' he echoed.

At that moment, a ferocious racket sounded above them, a snarling, yapping, howling, barking, roaring racket.

'The Gabriel Hounds,' Silver said, her voice low with dread. 'The Dodman's sending out the Gabriel Hounds.'

CHAPTER TWENTY-ONE
The Message

'Balthazar Mazurk!'

It was the Lord of the Wildwood who made the summons this time. The Queen sat on the fallen log, feeding her daughter. Behind her, Clive Arnold groaned in his enchanted sleep, one hand clenching and unclenching as if he fought an assailant in his dreams. She had thought that coming home to Eidolon would restore her health and her magic as well as her spirits, but nothing seemed to be going to plan. Isadora felt helpless, as if the Dodman had somehow managed to leach out of her whatever little power she had left. One dragon they had called had simply circled endlessly overhead, as if trying to withstand the summons with all its might; had briefly touched down, then flown away again – and she had not had the will to call it back. Another had landed, stared at her without saying a word, then attacked Xarkanadûshak, before retreating with a bitten wing.

And where were Ben and Darius? she wondered, for the hundredth time. Surely Ignatius could not have been so very hard to find? Perhaps the Wanderer had lived up to his name. Or more likely Ben had got carried away with exploring the Secret Country. Although Darius should know better. The annoyance she had been feeling had now turned to an anxiety nagging at the corners of her mind.

She was brought back to herself by the beat of wings over-head. A glorious flash of turquoise shimmered through the trees and the dragon Cernunnos had called slid in to land as silent as a ghost. It stood there gazing around at the gathered crowd, taking in the unexpected company with an air of contempt. Its cat-eyed gaze came to rest for a moment on the stag-headed man, then it transferred its attention to the quiet figure seated on the log.

It curled its lip.

'All this fuss,' it hissed, 'over such a feeble thing.'

The crest on its long neck rose in a line of frilled spikes and fanned back and forth: a magnificent array of jewelled lights.

Cernunnos looked alarmed. 'A feeble thing? To what do you refer?'

The dragon snorted. Then it reached out a foreleg and uncurled a single long claw which it pointed unerringly at

Isadora Arnold. 'Why, that feeble creature there! Such a hubbub everywhere about the returned Queen. I only came out of curiosity to have a look at it: had I wished to ignore your summons, I would have done so. No one commands the Great Mazurk!'

'You know very well that is not true,' Cernunnos countered. 'No one can resist the calling of their true name.' He flourished the Book of Naming and the dragon's eyes glittered at the sight of it.

'Well, if you're going to compel me, get on with it,' Balthazar Mazurk said proudly. 'But I can tell you, as soon as the compulsion wears off, you're toast.'

Behind the dragon, one of the fairies sniggered and whispered something to its neighbour. Without even bothering to look, the turquoise dragon twisted his head sharply and blew a stream of flame over its shoulder. Both fairies were instantly incinerated where they stood. The fern beneath which they had been sheltering remained completely untouched.

Wails of horror and distress rippled around the Wildwood clearing. Isadora shot to her feet. 'No!' she cried.

The dragon gave her a dismissive glance then stared defiantly at Cernunnos, as if waiting for a reprisal and the chance to show all those present exactly what he was capable of if provoked.

'That was uncalled for,' the Horned Man said, his face a mask of fury.

'That,' said Balthazar Mazurk with satisfaction, 'is how we

189

dragons deal with insolence. Take care you do not call down my fire on yourself.'

'Bad dragon.' Alice regarded the great turquoise creature solemnly. Then she wagged a finger at it, just like a grown-up. 'Bad!'

'*Ssh, ssh*,' her mother chided quickly, shielding her from the dragon's gimlet gaze with a protective arm, in case it decided to turn Alice into barbecued baby.

Xarkanadûshak stepped in front of his Queen and Alice. 'We need your help, Balthazar, in bringing the Eastern Clans to our side against the Dodman.'

'Why should we help you? We have problems of our own without getting involved in yours. The dinosaurs east of the Fire Mountains have united under a new leader and are trying to drive our clans out of our hereditary lands. The silly squabbles of the unwinged are of no concern while we have such matters to deal with. Unless –' and now his eyes glittered thoughtfully '– you do something for us first.'

'What do you wish of us?' Isadora asked.

'Use your Book to find the true name of the dinosaur's chief. Then we can summon him to a place of our choosing. And kill him.' Balthazar looked mightily pleased with himself for thinking of this brilliant plan. 'When we have done that, we will come and lend you our aid.'

The Queen looked shocked. 'I don't think—' she started.

But Cernnunos was already leafing through the Book of Naming. 'Ah, dinosaurs,' he muttered, finding the heading he was searching for. 'Now, what type of beast is this new leader?'

'A tyrannosaur,' Balthazar said eagerly. 'A rex. Tall fellow, walks upright, big teeth, mean little eyes—'

'Cernunnos!' the Queen burst out. She plonked Alice down on the ground and stepped forward. 'Stop at once. I command you!'

The stag-headed man stared at her in surprise. 'But we need the support of the dragons.'

'We cannot make such a bargain: it would not be right. To do such a treacherous thing would make us no better than those we seek to defeat. Now give me the Book.' And she laid hands firmly on the great leather volume.

The Lord of the Wildwood stared down at her, his face darkening, and he did not let go. For a moment it looked as if he would wrestle the Book of Naming from her grasp.

Balthazar Mazurk watched this interchange with narrowed eyes. His tail flicked up and down with annoyance. 'Tell me the name,' he wheedled. 'It's just a name . . .'

At that moment Ishtar appeared overhead, her scales gleaming in the moonlight. 'The Gabriel Hounds!' she warned as she swooped towards them. 'They are coming this way!' With a graceful sweep of her long wings she skimmed the treetops and soared up into the black sky again.

Balthazar Mazurk unfurled his wings. 'It is already too crowded here for my liking,' he said. 'And I have no wish to make the acquaintance of the Wild Hunt, or whoever drives them. Farewell.' He paused. 'Or not, as the case may be.'

Into the dark air he leapt and with two beats of his

powerful wings he was away, just as the eerie howls of the Hounds came cutting through the night.

As the Lord of the Wildwood stared up into the sky with apprehension, Isadora took the heavy great Book of Naming from his hands, laid it down beside her sleeping husband, arranged some moss over it and spoke two queer words. At once, man, book and moss blurred to a soft green mound, which would deceive the casual eye for a while, at least.

'Do you want me and Ishtar to see them off?' growled Zark, puffing out his chest.

Isadora picked up Baby Alice and smiled. 'You are very brave; but no: let us see why they come.'

'You should hide yourself, my lady,' Cernunnos said, taking her by the arm. 'We cannot afford to lose you.'

'I shall not run away,' the Queen said proudly. 'This is my home and I shall not hide in it. What sort of example would that be to my subjects? We must all face the thing we are afraid of or there is no hope of salvation.'

But even as she said this, she felt her heart beating like a trapped bird and realised she was terrified of seeing the Dodman again. A shiver of loathing ran through her marrow, but she straightened her spine and turned her face to the sky.

The Lord of the Wildwood ran a hand across his antlers as if testing his weapons before a fight. Then he sighed. 'Very well,' he said.

He made a gesture, and at once centaurs and dryads came out of the dark eaves of the Wildwood where they had been standing, ready to form a protective circle around their Queen;

fairies hovered in the trees; the other small creatures scattered for cover – but Jacaranda and the cats gathered at Isadora's feet.

Cernunnos regarded them with some amusement. 'The Gabriel Hounds are coming,' he reminded them. 'You cats had better make yourselves scarce.'

Jacaranda licked one of her paws nonchalantly and rubbed it upon her cheek. 'Oh, I think not,' she said, standing her ground. 'They are only ghost-dogs. We are too quick and clever for ordinary dogs – so what harm can their shades do us?'

Zark took several deep breaths, then turned away and surreptitiously blew upon a small pile of dry leaves, which ignited in a most satisfactory manner. While no one was watching, he stamped the flames out before they could catch hold. Then he fanned his wings and waited: if the Wild Hunt and their passengers gave the Queen any trouble they would have a real fire-breathing dragon to contend with!

Above them, the spectral hounds wheeled and dived, trailing a great chariot behind them. For a few seconds they disappeared amidst the forest canopy, and yelps and crashes could be heard as they descended; then a ghostly light penetrated the darkness, sending silvery fingers probing between the trees; and at last the Gabriel Hounds came into view: a pack of ghost-dogs, frost-white with fiery eyes, ghost-slobber dripping from their jaws, and the quiet of the Wildwood was shattered by their horrid howls. In the carriage they drew came a motley collection of creatures: but to Isadora's relief there was no dog-headed man amongst them.

Instead, a huge, ungainly creature clambered out of the carriage, flanked by a pair of goblins.

'Hello!' The giantess grinned around at the gathering good-naturedly, displaying her gruesome teeth. 'What a turnout: you've done us proud. I wuzzn't expecting a party!'

'State your business,' Cernunnos said sternly.

The giantess looked disappointed that matters should immediately get so formal: she'd been enjoying her new responsibility as an emissary; no one had ever asked her to do anything like this before.

'We brung a gift,' she said. 'From the Dodman.' She rummaged in her sack, discarding a handful of feathers, a claw covered in fluff, a scrap of fabric, a small skull with some fur still stuck on it, and finally came out with something small and rumpled and brightly coloured.

'And,' Bogie nudged her with a spiky elbow.

'And?' Grizelda frowned.

'The *message*,' he reminded her.

'Oh, the message.' Grizelda looked unhappy. She screwed her face up with the effort of memory. 'What message?' she asked after a long pause.

'Oh, for badness's sake!' exclaimed a voice which sounded unpleasantly like that of the Dodman.

Everyone in the clearing stopped what they were doing and looked around nervously, as if expecting the dog-headed man to materialise out of nowhere.

'*Squarrrk!*'

A bright-orange beak poked up out of the giantess's sack,

194

followed by a black head with a pair of beady eyes. The mynah bird clawed its way out of the bag, jumped up on to Grizelda's shoulder and stropped its beak briskly – once, twice, three times – on her leather jerkin. Then it fixed the Queen with its bright stare and said, sounding uncannily like its master, 'Your daughter Eleanor is most disappointed that you care so little for her that you have taken no 'eed of our last message. *Squarrrk!*'

Isadora frowned. Cernunnos glared at the bird as if the very power of his gaze could render it silent; but the mynah carried on cheerfully: 'You must come with us now if your daughter is to be saved. Ellie says –' and here it jumped up on to the giant-ess's head and hopped from one foot to the other '– "Oh, Mum, Mum, 'elp me!"' This it delivered in a horrible falsetto that sounded only a little like Ellie; but the ear-splitting shriek that it emitted after this plea made Mrs Arnold's hands fly up to her face in distress.

Grizelda and the bird regarded the Queen hopefully; then the mynah's attention was distracted by something interesting in the giantess's tangled mat of hair. Fixing one bright black eye on its prey, it pinpointed it, then stabbed down sharply with its beak. Grizelda yelped and shook her head, but the mynah bird wasn't going to be dislodged. Digging its claws in, it squinted down the length of its orange bill at the wormlike thing it had caught, flipped it carefully sideways and swallowed it with a single large gulp.

The giantess swatted at it with a huge hand and after a brief scuffle the bird lifted off, then took roost on her shoulder.

'So you see,' Grizelda said, remembering at last something of what she had been told to say. 'You must come with us, or Eleanor will die. You for her: that's the deal. And to show that he means business, the Dodman sends you this gift.'

And she handed the item to the Queen.

Mrs Arnold reached out her hands to take the 'gift' as if in a dream, but the Lord of the Wildwood snatched it away.

'Give me that!' Turning away from Isadora Arnold, he unwrapped it quickly and recoiled in disgust. 'What is this abomination?'

'Let me see!' The Queen's face was as white as a cloud, but her eyes were dark with anger.

'You don't want to see it,' Cernunnos began – but Mrs Arnold had swiped it with quick fingers.

'What on Eidolon is it?' she breathed.

'An ear, I believe,' the Horned Man said, gazing at the wizened, blackened, bloodstained thing in her hands.

Isadora's mouth twisted sharply as she examined the horrid object. 'An ear it may be, but an ear from no human, and it is certainly not Ellie's ear – quite aside from the fact that it's dark green, it's not even pierced, and I can't remember the last time Eleanor left the house without wearing earrings. That is certainly not my daughter's ear. But for some reason it is wrapped in Ellie's scarf, the scarf I bought her for her birthday last year. And just how did the Dodman lay his paws on *that*? I don't understand. I left Ellie behind in the Other World. Has the Dodman travelled there and stolen her in this short time?'

Cernunnos could not meet her eye.

'Does he hold my daughter captive?' she demanded of him grimly. 'Does he?'

The Lord of the Wildwood nodded unhappily.

'And you knew this?'

He opened his mouth to say something, thought better of it, and nodded again.

'You knew this and said nothing to me? Of my own daughter?' Two bright spots of pink had appeared on her pale cheeks: she looked absolutely furious. 'How could you keep such a thing from me, Cernunnos? How dared you?' And she drew herself up before him, transforming suddenly from devastated mother to regal queen.

The Lord of the Wildwood grimaced. 'How could I tell you? He wants you: it is the only reason he has taken your daughter, and if you give yourself up to him for her sake then we are all lost. Tell me, what choice did I have? I would not willingly have lied to you.'

Isadora gave him a hard look, then she transferred her gaze to the giantess. 'What is your name?'

Grizelda looked taken aback. 'Um, er . . .' She scratched her head. 'Ah . . .'

Bogie pinched her arm with his sharp little claws. 'It's Grizelda, you dolt!'

The giantess nodded happily. 'Grizelda,' she repeated.

The Queen looked impatient. 'Does the Dodman truly have my daughter, Grizelda?'

The giantess nodded vigorously.

'And she is still alive?'

'Um . . .'

'She is; yes, she is,' said the other goblin, hiding behind Grizelda's vast leg.

'And whose ear is this?' Isadora demanded.

The goblin sniggered. 'That's Bosko's, that is,' he said. 'Poor old Bosko. Now he's only got one.'

The Queen shook her head sadly. Such cruelty, even to a goblin . . . 'And if I come with you, he will let her go? Unharmed?'

'*Squarrrk!* If we bring you to the castle, Eleanor will be released. *Squarrk.* On this you have the Dodman's word. *Squarrrk!*'

'My lady, you cannot take the Dodman's word on this matter: he has no honour!' Cernunnos cried. 'If you go to him, what is to stop him from keeping you *both* captive?'

Isadora bowed her head, deep in thought. After a long pause she said, 'We must make the exchange. My life for my daughter's.'

A great sigh of distress swept around the clearing.

'My lady, you cannot!' The Lord of the Wildwood looked distraught.

'I must. And you, Cernunnos, must release Clive from his sleep and give Alice into his care. I had thought she would be safe here, but I see now that Eidolon is in a far more dangerous state then I had realised. I could not live with myself if anything were to happen to them.'

'By all means send the man and the child back to the

198

Other World,' Cernunnos said quietly. 'But if you are determined upon this course of action, then at least allow me and some others to accompany you, to ensure the exchange is made with honour and to bring the Princess Eleanor to safety.'

Isadora gave him a wan smile. 'Thank you, my friend.'

Then she raised her face to the sky.

'Ishtar!' she called.

Zark's wife suddenly planed above them like a great, exotic gull, wide wings outspread. Gracefully she swept down into the clearing and landed neatly beside her mate. The two dragons butted their heads together affectionately.

'I have a favour to ask you,' the Queen said. 'Can you carry my husband and Alice safely home to the Other World?'

'Of course.'

Her mate looked dubious. 'But—'

'No buts, Zark,' Isadora said briskly. 'It's the only way. I'd like to see it done now, so that my mind can be at rest.'

The Horned Man and the dragon exchanged a doleful glance, then Cernunnos bent and briefly touched Clive Arnold's forehead, muttering something under his breath.

Isadora's husband frowned in his sleep, grunted, and shrugged the Lord of the Wildwood's hand away. Turning on his side, he settled himself comfortably once more, and for a moment it looked as if he would never awaken again. Then his eyelids flickered and he groaned.

At once, Isadora was at his side. 'Clive, Clive, wake up!' she whispered urgently.

At last, he focused on her. A huge smile spread itself across his face. 'Darling—'

'You must get up now and take Alice home with you,' she said softly.

He frowned. 'Yes, of course. And you're coming home too?'

She smiled sadly. 'Yes,' she said. 'I shall be going home, too.'

Excellent!' He sat up and reached for his anorak, but before he had time to put it on or say anything else his wife had passed Alice to him.

'Ishtar and Jacaranda are going to accompany you.'

Alice clapped her hands. 'Izzie!' she declared. 'Ishtar!'

'Goodness,' said her father. 'That's a very fine word for a little girl.' And he looked fondly at his youngest daughter.

'Da! she said. 'Daddy!' And grabbed his nose.

'Ow!'

Mrs Arnold fixed her daughter with a firm, maternal gaze. 'Now, Alice,' she said. 'Just you behave: for me, and for Eidolon.'

'Eidolon,' Alice echoed, and beamed.

With his free hand Mr Arnold levered himself to his feet, and made his way over to the dragon, who was waiting with one shoulder dipped so that he could get on. His wife watched as he clambered awkwardly on to Ishtar with Baby Alice in his arms, and Jacaranda took up position at the base of the dragon's neck.

Alice never took her big green eyes off her mother. She waved her hands. 'Don't go,' she said suddenly. 'Not to the Dodman.'

Mr Arnold became very still. He looked at Alice; then he looked at his wife. 'What does she mean?' he exclaimed. 'Isadora—'

'Go!' the Queen implored Ishtar. 'Go, now!'

Whatever else Mr Arnold had to say was whisked away by the sound of the dragon's wings as she lifted into the air.

The Queen of Eidolon watched them until they were no more than a tiny speck in the night sky. She blinked rapidly, then ran the back of her hand across her eyes.

'Now, then, Grizelda,' she said briskly. 'You must return to your master and tell him that we will make the exchange: my life for my daughter's. At dawn I will be upon the lake shore which lies to the south of Corbenic Castle, and there I will await him. He must bring Eleanor there at first light, unharmed, and I will then give myself into his care at the same moment as he hands Ellie into the Lord of the Wildwood's care. This is the bargain I will make. Is that clear?'

The giantess gazed at her, almost cross-eyed with concentration. 'Dawn. Bring Eleanor, unharmed.'

'South shore. *Squarrrk!*' The mynah bird bobbed and whistled.

The goblin named Bogie caught the giantess's sleeve and tugged hard at it with his spiky little claws. 'No! We have to take her back with us. That's what Old Dog-Head said: "Bring me the Queen, or I will eat your livers". That's what he said!'

Grizelda looked puzzled. 'He can eat my liver: I don't much like it, personally. Nice bit of stegosaur-steak-and-kidney pie, now that's a different matter, but liver – yuk!'

Bogie rolled his eyes. 'Nah, stupid. He meant *our* livers.' And he poked his finger into her capacious abdomen. 'That liver: he'll hoick it out and fry it up!'

The other goblin shuddered. 'He won't even stop to cook it,' it said, grimacing.

Now the giantess began to look concerned. '*My* liver?' she echoed. 'He's going to eat *my* liver?' She shook her head, laughed; gave Brimstone a massive wink. 'You're having me on.' And she gave him a good-natured punch on the arm that sent him flying in amongst the hounds, who all ran around and around one another, yapping and snarling. It looked as if a full-scale fight might break out at any moment.

Queen Isadora watched these antics in consternation. Could she entrust such a delicate bargain to such idiots? she wondered. That Ellie should be in the hands of creatures like these – who might do her harm without even understanding what they did – made her shudder. Then she reminded herself that all of them were her subjects: like it or not, they were all Eidolon's folk.

And so she raised her voice and cried, 'Go, now! Take this message back to your master without delay!'

At the sound of her voice, the Gabriel Hounds fell abruptly silent and immediately stood in line, haunches quivering. The two goblins shot her a look of surprise and scrambled into the cart. The mynah bird took off from Grizelda's shoulder, squawking loudly, 'Message to the master! South shore at dawn. Bring Eleanor unharmed. *Squarrrrk!*'

And at last the giantess turned around, got into the back of the chariot and sat down with such a thump that the whole frame shuddered and threatened to break apart.

A moment later they were gone, up into the lightening air.

Cernunnos and the Queen, and every creature of the Wildwood, or those summoned from beyond it, watched as the Wild Hunt was swallowed by the darkness – and dread showed on every upturned face.

CHAPTER TWENTY-TWO

Rescue

Without a thought for the goblin guards, Ben hurtled around the corner and out into the candlelit corridor, shouting at the top of his voice, 'Ellie! Ellie, where are you?'

Silver and Iggy hesitated no more than a second, then ran out after him, with Darius clattering along behind them.

Skerry rolled his eyes. 'So much for secrecy,' he said. He shook the little wood-sprite. 'Where is she, then?' he asked it. 'I know you know.'

Acorn's mouth twisted. 'I was supposed to fetch help; though this wasn't quite what I had in mind.' He laughed bitterly. 'If I tell you, will you help me get out of here?'

The big selkie regarded him with his lucent blue gaze until Acorn felt a hot wash of shame flush through him. 'Follow me,' he said, and flittered out into the corridor.

At first the goblins couldn't quite believe their eyes. Out of the shadows, where there really shouldn't have been anything at all except perhaps a few spiders and maybe a couple of fire-fairies, came a yelling elf-boy, a cat, and a girl with flying hair and silvery-grey eyes. Any one of these on their own might have provided welcome sport and a much-needed midnight snack: but all three at once was quite a different prospect.

For a moment they dithered: then a centaur came charging into view.

Grabbit and Gutty exchanged a look of round-eyed panic then took to their heels, their game of knucklebones discarded in a flurry. 'Help!' they cried. 'Help! We're under attack!'

'Come back, you cowards!' Ben yelled after them. 'Tell me where my sister is!'

But the goblins weren't stopping for anything.

'This way.'

The voice – scratchy and light – came from above. Ben looked up to find Acorn hovering over him in a blur of wings.

'I know where she is.' He paused, blinking. 'Or was.'

Up stairs, around corners, down draughty passageways and along corridors down which he had only recently flown in fear for his life, Acorn led them with his heart in his mouth. What if the Dodman had killed the Princess? What if he was still there?

But when he reached his destination, the corridor was dark and empty, the only visible movement the guttering of the last candle-flame jumping across the walls.

'Ellie! Ellie!' Ben shouted.

His cry fell into a profound silence; then: 'Ben?'

The voice came from behind the third door. It quavered with disbelief. Then there was a scuffle of movement and more loudly it called, 'Ben, is that really you?'

'It is! It is!' Ben almost laughed with relief. But his euphoria was short-lived. Ellie might be alive, but she was behind a locked door. He pushed at the door again, thumped it, kicked it; to no avail.

'Stand aside,' Darius said. He waited until his friends were out of the way, then he reared up on his great haunches and brought his hooves crashing down on the door.

The timber shuddered and rattled, but the door wasn't budging an inch. Again and again he thrashed at it, but all he managed was to dent and splinter the surface and make a din. And when Skerry tried to shoulder the door in, all he got for his efforts was a big splinter in his arm.

'Now what?' Ben asked.

'We need the keys,' Silver groaned, and the two of them looked at one another in despair.

On the other side of the door, Ellie began to cry.

'How very interessssting!'

'It is indeed.'

Cynthia's voice was thoughtful as she observed from her

vantage point, in the dark branches of a great oak some distance south of the clearing, how the lumbering giantess and the two goblins climbed back into the chariot after delivering what appeared to be some sort of message. A moment later, the Gabriel Hounds were howling again, their cries ululating through the Wildwood, echoing off the trees, filling the night with their din.

Then she watched as the Lord of the Wildwood wrapped a fur cloak about the Queen's shoulders and gathered the centaurs. She watched as Isadora mounted one of the horse-men, and Cernunnos led a solemn procession out of the Wildwood, accompanied overhead by a lone, forlorn-looking dragon.

Soon the first hint of dawn was beginning to strike through the darkness, the edge of the rising sun sending a deep-red glow into the blackness of the sky as if a forest fire was raging in the distant hills.

'Red sssky in the morning, Dodman'sss warning!' hissed the Sphynx, as if reading her mind. Its breath misted briefly in the chilly air.

'I am very curious,' Cynthia declared, 'as to exactly what is happening here.'

The Sphynx grinned, baring its long yellow teeth. Sometimes, Cynthia thought, it looked more like a rat than a cat, with its naked coat and skinny tail. It was one of the things she liked most about it. That, and its ability to sneak around unseen.

'Go and have a look, see if you can find out what is going on,' she told it. 'You're such a clever little spy.'

'Yesss,' agreed the hairless cat. 'I am.'

It licked the last smell of the terrible troll off its skin and stretched out its back legs, then its front legs. Then it ran straight up the trunk of an oak, digging its long claws into the bark for purchase – and the oak twitched and muttered in the deep, secret voice of trees in all worlds when they are upset by something; until the cat ran out along a branch and leapt neatly on to the outstretched limb of a nearby ash. In this manner it soon vanished from its mistress's sight into the dark mass of the Wildwood.

Cynthia sat back amongst the ferns, thinking. The Queen had not been wearing the Crown of Eidolon when she went with the centaur and the Horned Man; nor had she been carrying a suitcase, nor the baby. Many possibilities flickered through her head as she waited for the Sphynx to return with whatever news it had been able to glean.

She did not have to wait for too long before the hairless cat was back, its amber eyes flashing maliciously in the weird light.

'A new day isss dawning for Eidolon,' the Sphynx reported gleefully. 'The Queen hasss gone to give herself up to the Dodman in exchange for young Ellie.'

Cynthia's straggly orange eyebrows shot up into her straggly orange hair. She stroked her long, crooked nose with a long and crooked finger. 'Well, well,' she said. 'That's very curious.'

'And,' the hairless spy added, its yellow grin as wide as a goblin's, 'they have left something very interesssting behind.'

And when he told her what it was, Cynthia's grin soon matched his own.

*

'Right, then,' Darius said firmly, sounding a good deal more confident than he felt. 'Skerry and I will go and find the keys.'

'But,' came Ellie's voice on the other side of the cell door, 'the Dodman's got them. Oh, please help me: it's as black as the grave in here and I'm afraid of the dark.' It was a big admission for Ellie. She started to sob again.

The big selkie rubbed his face. 'I'm sorry. I only came along for the ride,' he said slowly. 'Confronting the Dodman wasn't what I had in mind.'

Darius gave him a hard look. 'Go, then,' he said. 'Take your daughter and go back to your safe waters. Though I warn you that unless we can rescue Eleanor and stop the Dodman's plan, they will not remain safe for very long.'

Skerry nodded. 'You're right, of course, I know. But I've never regarded myself as any kind of hero. I like a quiet life: ride the occasional good wave, eat a few fish, catch some rays – that sort of thing.'

'Dad . . .' Silver stepped in front of him. Her face looked fierce and her eyes flashed in the gloom of the corridor as if lit with some inner light. 'Ben saved my life when I was taken into the Other World. We owe him this. And if you won't go with Darius, then I will.'

Her father looked abashed. He gazed at her out of the depths of his big blue eyes as if seeing her for the first time. At last he grinned. 'Well, I really wouldn't be much of a father, let alone a hero, if I let you go instead of me.' He gave her a hug, winked over her head at Ben. 'Look after her, won't you?'

Ben nodded.

Skerry pushed Silver away, ruffled her hair, then turned to the centaur. 'Lead on, Darius. Lead on.'

The centaur paused. 'Take heart, Eleanor,' he said, bending to speak into the keyhole. 'We'll get you out of here, I promise, by hoof or by tooth.'

Ben could feel his sister's smile, even though they were separated by a thick wooden door and walls of sturdy stone; then the centaur and the selkie were gone into the shadows, the sound of the Horse Lord's hooves ringing on the stone.

Silver watched them go, looking even paler than usual. 'What if they don't come back? What if they get captured – or worse? What will we do?'

Ben squeezed her hand. He was glad she was a girl at the moment, because squeezing her hand was the only comfort he could think of, and squeezing a flipper wouldn't have been quite the same.

Ignatius Sorvo Coromandel rubbed his cheek against her leg. 'Don't take on,' he rasped in his best tiger-growl, 'nothing bad is going to happen while the Wanderer's here to take care of you.'

Ben and Silver looked down at the really rather small cat and burst out laughing.

'It's all right for you,' came Ellie's voice. 'You can laugh all you want: you're not stuck in some horrible dungeon with nothing but a smelly bucket for company.'

That sobered them. 'Sorry, Ellie,' Ben said through the keyhole. 'Are you okay?'

'No, I'm not. It's dark and I've got a headache and I've been sick.'

'We heard an awful scream earlier,' Ben went on. 'I was worried it was you.'

'I think the Dodman did something to one of his goblins.' There was a shuffling noise on the other side of the door, then something gleamed through the keyhole. 'Oh, I can see you!' Ellie exclaimed with sudden delight. 'Who's that with you?'

'This is She Who Swims the Silver Path of the Moon,' Ben said proudly. 'But she prefers to be called Silver. She's a selkie.'

'Hello,' said Silver.

'Hello. You don't look much like a seal,' Ellie said, thus surprising Ben by knowing anything about the subject at all. He had thought she only ever read magazines about how to attract boys by wearing glittery purple eyeshadow and dieting till you looked like a wizened old stick – which had always seemed a deeply unlikely way of getting anyone's attention, unless you wanted them to laugh at you. 'Oh, hello, is that you, Acorn?'

The wood-sprite circled around Ben's head. 'I brought them,' he said. Which was neither entirely true nor yet entirely untrue.

'Thank you, Acorn. Thank you from the bottom of my heart.'

If wood-sprites could blush, Acorn would have done so then. 'It was nothing,' he mumbled.

'It's terribly dark in here without you,' Ellie said miserably. 'It's easier to keep your spirits up if you've got a little light.'

'What about the fire-fairies?' Ben said suddenly,

remembering the tiny light-headed creatures in the caverns below. 'Acorn, do you think you could persuade a couple of them to come up here and slip in through the keyhole to give Ellie some light?' He reckoned they were small enough, and since if they could get in they could get out again, it wasn't as if they'd be in too much danger.

'Maybe,' said Acorn, though he didn't sound very keen on the idea.

'Please,' said Ellie. She paused, then added in a small voice, 'Unless you could manage to squeeze back in here?'

Iggy laughed cruelly. 'I don't think there'd be much left of him if we tried to cram him through that keyhole!'

That made Acorn's mind up for him. Away down the corridor he flitted, a zigzag of pale-green light which disappeared as soon as he rounded the first corner.

'Do you think he'll come back?' said Silver.

Ben looked at her in surprise. 'Of course he will.' But it was true that the wood-sprite didn't seem as friendly as Twig. He watched Ignatius Sorvo Coromandel wander off to sniff at the door of the next cell.

'There's someone in here,' Iggy said, recoiling suddenly with a sneeze. 'And they don't half smell!'

'I heard that,' Ellie said. 'Don't be so rude! That's my friend, the minotaur.'

As if in response to this introduction, there came a tremendous bellow from the adjoining cell.

'Oh!' Silver jumped behind Ben, trembling. 'The minotaur! Don't let him get me!'

Ben frowned. He'd read a story about a minotaur, a Greek myth about a hero called Theseus, who had sailed to Crete with a group of young people who were to be that year's sacrifice to the beast; and somehow – the details of the story were a bit hazy – he had survived the ordeal, killed the minotaur and found his way back out of the maze in which it was kept. Oh, and won the heart of the King's daughter, though that wasn't the bit that interested Ben very much. Killing the monster had been the fun bit of the story, scary and exciting. However, he didn't feel much like taking on a real life minotaur. He was glad it was securely imprisoned, even if Ellie said it was her friend.

'Don't worry, Silver, he can't get you; and I won't let him.'

Silver beamed up at him. 'You are my hero, Ben.'

Ben blushed to the roots of his hair. He was saved from further embarrassment by the sound of footsteps coming down the stairs. He looked at the selkie in panic. 'We must hide!'

But there wasn't anywhere to hide. They couldn't run back the way they had come without being seen as they passed the stairs, and the corridor on which Ellie's cell was located came to a dead end beyond them.

'Stay here, Silver. I'll go and see who it is. If I shout, run as fast as you can back the way we came, and I'll hold them up so you can get away,' Ben whispered, trying to sound braver than he felt.

He and Iggy ran along the corridor to the junction with the stairs. There they stopped. The footsteps were coming closer. More than one set. Ben counted. Three sets, at least, striking against stone, the echoes making it sound like even more. He felt his heart clench. He and Iggy exchanged worried glances, then Ben stuck his head around the corner and stared upwards. At first he could see nothing, then . . .

'Skerry!'

The relief was so great that his knees went all wobbly.

Behind the selkie came Darius. As soon as Ben saw his face he knew something was badly wrong. 'What? What is it?'

'The doors up above are locked. We couldn't get through.'

'So you haven't got the keys, then?' said Ben in a quiet voice.

Skerry fixed his great blue eyes on him. 'I'm sorry, Ben. We've done all we could, and now there's no more to be done. I'll take Silver now and we'll away. I'm sorry about your sister.'

'Darius?'

But the Horse Lord just shook his head slowly. He looked utterly dejected. 'When they built this place, they built it well,' he said. 'The doors are locked and bound with iron. If I could take the walls down stone by stone to save your sister, I would, Ben, believe me. Short of swimming around to the front of the castle and declaring war on the Dodman, I don't know what we can do.'

No one said anything to this. No one had any ideas. Ben felt as if the inside of his head had been scoured out and left as empty and echoing as an old kettle. He looked from the unhappy faces of the centaur and the selkies away into the shadows of the corridor.

There, at the far end, something lit the gloom. Ben stared and stared. Then he fixed his Eidolon eye upon the distant

215

glow. It was Acorn and a great swarm of fire-fairies, coming closer by the second.

Well, he thought, *at least Ellie will have some light to comfort her*. It wasn't much consolation, but it was something.

'Thank you, Acorn,' he said as they approached. 'Thank you, fire-fairies.'

The fire-fairies jigged about his head, making mad zigzags of bright light in front of his eyes, buzzing like little bees full of joyous energy, and suddenly Ben couldn't help but smile, despite the dire situation they were all in.

'Follow me,' he said, and they all streamed along behind him like a golden cloak.

When they reached Ellie's cell, the fire-fairies first flew in a stream of gold around Iggy, then around Silver, and then they danced up and down the door, then round and round, in what seemed a very disorganised sort of manner. But none of them went through the keyhole. They flew above it and below it, to the left and the right of it, but not one of them went in. Ben couldn't really blame them for not wanting to enter one of the Dodman's dungeons; even so, it was very frustrating to watch them having fun in their carefree, thoughtless way.

'What are they doing?' Silver asked Acorn, but the wood-sprite shook its head.

'They are as much of a mystery to me as they are to you,' he said in his scratchy little voice.

'Well, you must have said something to them to make them come.'

Acorn looked uncomfortable. 'I only got as far as explaining that the Princess of Eidolon was trapped up here, then they were flying so fast I could hardly keep up with them.'

A great hum filled the air, as if all the fire-fairies had started to sing a single note at once; then there was a sudden blast of light accompanied by a strong smell of burning and something went clattering on to the stonework in a great cloud of dust.

Silver sneezed hard, and Ben's eyes watered from all the dust and light. He blinked and blinked; then he stared.

Where the great iron lock had been, there was now a burnt and ragged hole in the cell's door; and through it he could see Ellie clearly, with a dozen or more fire-fairies zooming around her, weaving patterns of light in the shadows about her head – a pattern which looked remarkably like a crown . . .

He burst out laughing, for now the door was swinging open and there were fire-fairies everywhere, making the cell as bright as day.

'Oh, Ellie!' he cried, and then he was hugging his sister and she was hugging him – which was pretty strange, because generally they didn't even *like* one another most of the time.

Darius and Skerry gazed at the burnt-out lock, then at Ellie embracing her brother, and finally at what now appeared to be a dual crown of fire-fairies which hovered over them.

'Well, I never . . .' The centaur shook his head so that his glossy black mane of hair tossed from side to side. 'I thought I knew everything there was to know about the creatures of this world, but somehow they are always surprising me.'

Skerry's huge laugh boomed out. 'Task accomplished, then,

and by the smallest of Eidolon's folk: so much for our brains and brawn, my friend!'

Darius smiled. His gaze met Ellie's, and at once she blushed and started fiddling with her hair. 'I must look awful . . .' she started.

Ben rolled his eyes. 'Come on, then,' he said impatiently, catching his sister by the arm. 'Let's get out of here.'

Ellie pulled herself free. 'Not without the minotaur.'

Darius stared at her. '*Here?* The minotaur is here?'

'If he is, he's best left here,' Skerry said, frowning. 'He's got a lot to answer for.'

'He's been very nice to me,' Ellie said.

'No doubt biding his time,' said the selkie darkly.

Darius looked anxious. 'He is very dangerous, and very powerful. If we get him out, how can we be sure he won't hurt anyone?'

'Simple,' said Ellie briskly. 'I'll make him promise.'

Ben made a face. 'Listen to Princess Ellie.'

For once, his sister did not rise to the bait, but walked straight past him to the door of the next cell. 'Minotaur?'

A heavy sigh issued from behind the door. 'You're free, then? Good for you. Maybe we'll meet again. Or maybe we won't. It's been nice knowing you –' it paused '– Princess of Eidolon.'

Ellie loved the sound of that.

'If we help you to escape your cell, will you promise not to hurt anyone?'

'Anyone?'

'Well, any of my friends.' She cast Ben a superior look which said, *so you'd better behave from now on . . .*

There was a brief silence while the minotaur digested this. Then it said quietly, 'If you can get me out of here, I will do anything in the world for you.'

Ellie clapped her hands in delight. Then she turned to Darius. 'You see?'

'If you believe that you'll believe anything,' Acorn said darkly.

Skerry walked over and caught Silver by the hand. 'If that thing runs amok, there's nothing I'll be able to do to stop it, and I won't risk my daughter's life needlessly.'

'No! I won't leave Ben!' Silver pulled away, but the big selkie was adamant.

'Ben may be your friend, but I am your father.' He turned to Darius. 'We will wait for you in the waters of the caves below. And if you do not come, well –' he shrugged '– at least as seals we can save ourselves.'

The little selkie's huge eyes started to brim with tears.

'You'd better go, Silver,' Ben said rather miserably. He hung his head, wondering if this was the last time he would ever see her.

As if she shared his thought, she broke suddenly from her father's grasp, ran to Ben's side and kissed him quickly on the cheek. Then she turned and ran with Skerry down the corridor and disappeared into the shadows.

'Well, well,' said Ellie. 'Ben's got a girlfriend!'

Ben put his hand up to his cheek. It felt hot and red where

Silver had kissed him. 'I have not!' he denied furiously. But he could feel a smile bubbling up inside him.

'Come now,' said the centaur. 'No time for bickering. We must away as fast as possible, with the minotaur or without him. What's it to be?' He turned to Ben.

'Let him out,' said Ben as bravely as he could manage, though he was a bit worried, and not just by the beast's smell. But nothing should be kept down here, in the dark and the damp. 'Acorn, can you ask the fire-fairies?'

But before he could even finish the sentence, the fire-fairies had flown to the door of the next cell and were already working their strange magic.

As the burnt-out lock fell away and the door swung open, Ignatius Sorvo Coromandel gazed into the cell and his eyes went huge and round. Then he fled down the corridor and leapt into Ben's arms.

Ben didn't even have time to chide him for his cowardice before a huge figure ducked through the door, to emerge in a swirl of smoke and dust and fire-fairies; and then he couldn't even speak if he'd wanted to. A vast, rumbling bellow roiled out across the dungeons and echoed off the walls, and the sound thrummed in the bones of Ben's chest and up through the soles of his feet.

Golden light from the fairies and the dancing candles illuminated a creature as tall as the Dodman, walking on two legs like any man. But when he examined it with his Eidolon eye, Ben found that its head was the head of the biggest bull in any world, topped by a pair of monstrous black horns.

What Ben wanted to do when he saw this apparition was to run away: to pound along the corridor and down all those flights of stairs up which they had climbed, down into the caves and into the pool where Melusine and Skerry and Silver waited; and then swim the lake without anyone else's help at all until he was as far away from the minotaur as he could possibly get. What he actually did, though, was to stand rooted to the spot, barely breathing, with his arms clutched tightly around the little cat and his eyes as big as dinner plates.

'Wow . . .!'

Even Darius gulped, and his voice sounded a bit shaky when he said, 'Welcome back to the world, minotaur. May I remind you that you are now in the service of the Queen of Eidolon.'

The minotaur slowly swung his huge head to survey the centaur with eyes of flame. 'I am in the service of the Princess Eleanor,' he rumbled, 'and no other.'

At this, a dozen of the fire-fairies circled around him, tracing in the dark air a golden, floating heart.

Which made Ellie's eyes shine, even though her knees were knocking.

CHAPTER TWENTY-THREE

Red Dawn

When the Dodman saw that the chariot drawn by the Wild Hunt did not contain the woman he had sent his messengers to fetch, he flew into a rage. Goblins scattered into dark corners of the castle, vampire chickens fluttered up to the rafters in a storm of feathers, and the white wolves who had once answered only to the call of the Horned Man slunk into the shadows with their tails between their legs and their ears laid flat to their skulls. Even the guard-trolls on the gate stood stock-still and pretended they were lumps of stone, in the hope he would not take his fury out on them.

Bogie and Brimstone had been preparing for this fearful

223

prospect ever since they had left the Wildwood without the Queen. They had even made the Wild Hunt fly round and round in circles so they could think of a way to avoid their master's wrath. In the end all they had been able to fix on was this: 'Leg it!'

As soon as the Gabriel Hounds landed, the two goblins were out of the chariot and scampering across the courtyard as fast as their fat little legs could carry them, leaving Grizelda to face the Dodman. Even so, they managed to somehow get tangled up in one another and fall flat on their faces.

The Dodman was upon them in a flash, planting a foot squarely on each goblin's back as if he would crush them into the ground.

'Where is she?' he boomed, and they could hear the spittle flying from his mouth and sizzling on to the cobblestones.

Unfortunately, he was standing on them so heavily that they could not get any words out, which just made him angrier.

'WHERE . . . IS . . . SHE?'

With each word he stamped down hard, and groans of air came out of the goblins in such a rude manner that Grizelda started to giggle. She was still stuffing her fingers into her mouth in order (unsuccessfully) to stifle her laughter when the Dodman abandoned the two squashed goblins – who lay there for a few moments, looking rather flattened, before levering themselves to their feet and making their escape – and launched himself at her. Three inches away, he drew himself up and looked her squarely in the eye – which, given the size of a giantess, is no mean feat, even if you are eight-foot tall with the head of a dog.

'Where . . . is . . . the . . . Queen?' he enunciated with great care, remembering that he was addressing a creature with a very small brain, despite the size of the rest of her.

Grizelda gave him a gap-toothed, lopsided smile. 'With the Horned Man,' she said. 'In the Wildwood.'

The Dodman's breath hissed out in a dangerous fashion.

Even the Gabriel Hounds quietened, sensing the storm about to explode. But before the Dodman could lose his temper entirely and tear everyone present limb from limb, the mynah bird burst out of the giantess's pack and circled overhead, squawking: 'Bring the Princess Eleanor to the south shore at dawn. Unharmed! Unharmed!'

The Dodman regarded the creature with a look that suggested if he got hold of it at least one person would be eating mynah bird that day, and that person probably had a lot of very sharp dog's teeth.

'Go on,' he told it. 'Then what?'

'The Queen will give herself up to you. That is her bargain.'

Everyone waited, not daring to breathe, as they awaited the dog-headed man's response.

At last, a calculating look slicked the Dodman's eyes. 'Excellent,' he said, rubbing his hands together. 'That will do very well.'

His grin was as long and gleaming as any crocodile's. He crossed the courtyard to look through one of the narrow arrow-slits in the stone walls there. To the north of the castle, all was quiet and dark; but to the east, the first glimmers of red light had begun to enrich the night sky; and when he reached the southern wall and peered into the murky distance, he thought he could make out a group of figures emerging from the treeline there.

At once, he was all spring and vigour. 'Right then, Brimstone, Bogie, Bosko, Batface!' he cried briskly to the hiding goblins. 'Down to the dungeons. Let us fetch the Princess Eleanor and make our trade!'

He chased the goblins out of the shadows and they fled before him, one of them sporting a ragged bandage around its head, the others averting their eyes and trying to keep out of range of their master's booted feet. His moods were changeable at the best of times, and who knew when he would feel like taking off someone else's ear?

As he danced lightly down the steep stone stairs to the dungeons with the keys rattling merrily at his side, he sang to himself:

'*We're going to catch a queen, tra-la*
With eyes of emerald-green, tra-la
Going to lock her in the cells, tra-la
Full of lovely minotaur smells, tra-la
Going to take away her crown, tra-la
Bring the whole world crashing down
Tra-la, tra-la, tra-la, la, la!'

'Oh my, it's the Dodman!'

Ellie looked fearfully at her brother. Ben stared at the locked door above them. The Dodman had the keys . . .

'Right, that's it,' Acorn declared, flittering above their heads.

'I'm off. I'm not staying around here to be caught by the Dodman again.'

But no one seemed to be listening to him.

Darius glanced at the door, then at the minotaur. If anything could hold them at bay, it would be this monster; though how the dog-headed man had ever managed to capture it in the first place, he couldn't imagine.

'We must do everything in our power to protect the Princess Eleanor and her brother,' he said to the minotaur, who nodded his bull-head in assent.

Then Darius turned to Ben. 'Take your sister and Ignatius down to the caves and join the selkies,' he said urgently. 'Get them to take you across the lake as fast as they can. The minotaur and I will follow when we are able.'

'No!' Ben said fiercely. 'We won't leave you to fight our battles.'

The minotaur swung his gaze in Ellie's direction. 'You should do as the man-horse says. We will deal with the Dog-Headed One and his minions.' His eyes gleamed. Then he pawed the ground, just as a bull might, except that his feet were those of a very large man. 'I have been looking forward to this moment. It has been a long time coming.'

Ellie paled, but she didn't want to appear scared in front of the handsome centaur or her new friend. 'We're staying,' she said, though her voice wobbled a little.

Ignatius Sorvo Coromandel gave her a ferocious grin. 'I've got a few scores of my own to settle with the Dodman. I've been polishing up my claws especially.'

The sound of footsteps were coming closer on the other side of the door. Keys jangled. Everyone held their breath and stared at the huge ironbound door.

It was a huge affair made from ancient oak-wood, its surface pitted with age and wear, its long hinges and ringed handle rusted but sturdy. Scorchmarks and clefts marred the wood, as if the door had survived through centuries of violent events. Ben hoped it would stand for a few minutes more.

The minotaur grabbed hold of the iron ring and took a firm stance. Darius arched his strong neck so that the tendons stood out on it like cords. Ben clenched his fists and listened to the sound of his heart thudding against his ribs. Ellie bit her lip.

At the sound of the Dodman approaching with the Gabriel Hounds howling and yapping and snuffing hungrily behind him, Iggy's hackles rose into spikes all the way down his spine and his tail fluffed up alarmingly, like an animal all of its own. All this time he had been thinking, for all his bravado, that if it really did come down to teeth-and-claw fighting he might just run away. Now he felt his fur puffing up all over, so that his shadow loomed large against the door, and he began to feel a bit brave after all. Fighting chemicals poured into him, swelling his muscles – and probably his head, too. The mighty Wanderer had returned.

The minotaur swung his great head around to look at his new allies. His eyes gleamed red as flame; but perhaps it was just the reflection of the fire-fairies.

'Get ready, then,' he said.

He did not say for what: he did not have to. The key turned in the door.

As the sun came up over the eastern hills behind Corbenic Castle, Queen Isadora of Eidolon stood on the lake shore with Cernunnos, Lord of the Wildwood, and a phalanx of centaurs. She scanned the castle avidly, one hand shielding her eyes from the gaudy light.

'Red sky in the morning, dryads' warning,' Cernunnos intoned, but whether this meant it was a warning to dryads or from them, Isadora did not know. All she did know was that the castle looked ominous and bleak, silhouetted against that glowing red sky. And there was no sign of the Dodman or her daughter anywhere.

Xarkanadûshak planed overhead like a hawk. He sideslipped across the lake, risking a swift pass over the castle battlements, then returned and landed gracefully beside them, shaking his head.

'I can't see anyone,' he reported. 'But there's a lot of noise coming from inside the castle somewhere, and the Gabriel Hounds are barking like demons.'

'Perhaps Ellie has escaped,' Isadora breathed. She turned shining green eyes on the Lord of the Wildwood.

'There's no way out except across the lake,' said Cernunnos. 'And I fear that if the Wild Hunt are pursuing your daughter in the confines of the castle walls, it could be a very grim end.'

Isadora shuddered. She knew how hounds dealt with foxes when they caught them in the Other World, and it was a violent, bloody death. Tears threatened. She grasped Cernunnos by the arm. 'We have to help her. I must go.' She turned to the dragon. 'Zark, you could carry me—'

'No!' Cernunnos took her by the shoulders, blocking her view of the castle. 'If you go to him, he will have both of you, and where is the sense in that?'

There was nothing she could do. Being Queen of this world seemed to confer on her no special powers. What was the use of being a queen if you could not even save your own daughter? She hung her head and waited.

The Lord of the Wildwood narrowed his eyes. Perhaps if the Princess Eleanor were to suffer a grim fate at the hands and teeth of the Dodman and his monsters it would be best for all: Isadora would remain with him in the safety of the Wildwood, a rallying point for the creatures of Eidolon – more of whom would surely flock to her side in sympathy at the loss of her daughter. He could not help the small smile which twitched his lips.

The key turned in the lock, and someone pushed hard on the door – but it did not open. From the other side came muffled swearing followed by a yelp as a goblin was bashed for handing up the wrong key. More rattling. Another key in the lock, and a quiver as the door was pushed hard. Still no luck. The minotaur's arms bulged. He dropped the centaur a slow wink.

'The Dog-Headed One will have to try harder than that,' he said softly. 'On his own he is a feeble creature, for all his size.

You should all remember that. It is only by terrorising others into his service that he gains his power.'

On the other side of the door, there was considerable puzzlement.

'There's an appalling stench coming from somewhere,' the Dodman declared disgustedly, wrinkling his big black nose. 'Is it you, Bosko? Have you been eating rat droppings again?'

Bosko denied this vehemently (though he had).

'I know what that smell is,' said Grizelda. 'I should do: I dragged that net for miles, me and the ogres Oddspot and Offside. Over hill and down dale. I'll never forget it.'

'What?' The Dodman was sorting through the keys again, frowning at the first one – which he just knew was the right one, even though it didn't appear to work.

'It's the minotaur,' the giantess went on. 'I'd know that smell anywhere . . .'

The Dodman's head came up sharply. 'The minotaur? But he's imprisoned safe and sound next to the Princ—

He bent suddenly, withdrew the latest ill-fitting key from the lock and applied his eye to the enormous keyhole. The next moment, he leapt backwards with a look of utmost fury on his face.

'He's got out!' He glared at the goblins, who quailed away as if the heat in his eyes alone might sear them to little piles of ash. 'And so has the Princess. But I locked her cell, I know I did!' He peered through the keyhole again. 'And that little brat of a brother is with her! How did THAT happen?'

His fearsome gaze raked them all. The Gabriel Hounds

began to whimper and their tails drooped and quivered. One of the goblins wet himself.

'Well? WELL?' he bellowed.

'Dunno,' Bosko muttered, feeling the furious gaze upon him.

'No idea.'

'Search me.'

'Magic?'

'MAGIC?' The Dodman's boot found the last speaker, connecting with its large rump with an audible *squelch*. 'Don't use that word around me! Well, however this fiasco has occurred we'll soon put it to rights. And then I shall have *two* little hostages to play with. That should make Isadora come squealing to me for mercy. Grizelda: open that door!'

The giantess looked dubious, but she did what she was told. Or tried. She battered at the door with her fists, wrenched at the iron ring, tried to shoulder it open. A tiny crack of fiery light appeared down the edge on her last, most violent attempt.

'Hah!' cried the Dodman. 'Put your back into it, woman!'

Grizelda pulled a face. Then she turned around and slowly applied her capacious bottom to the door, pushing backwards as hard as she could. It creaked and creaked, and the fiery line grew wider. This time a couple of the fire-fairies buzzed through it, zooming over the Dodman's head, away and up the stairs into the glowing dawn. A moment later, Acorn levered himself through and followed them.

On the other side, Ellie shrieked. With a massive heave, the minotaur slammed the door fully shut again with a clang.

Now the goblins, with the Wild Hunt snapping at their heels and other more vulnerable regions, joined the giantess in pushing the door open – and it gave by an inch, and then another inch.

With a roar, the minotaur shoved it closed; but as he did so the Dodman's words drifted with horrible clarity through the gap.

'This calls for a dragon. If brute force won't solve the problem, then fire must!'

'Oh, no,' breathed Ben, as the door slammed shut again.

'A dragon . . .' said Iggy. 'Now *that* would be bad.' Abruptly, his fur subsided and he looked no longer like the mighty Wanderer, but like the small, frightened cat that he was.

'Take the children,' the minotaur said sharply, addressing the centaur. 'I will hold the door.'

'But—'

'Do not argue with me, horse-man.' The minotaur's eyes glinted dangerously. 'You never know what I might do.'

Darius conceded to himself that this was true. It was hard to trust a beast with such a bloodthirsty reputation. He turned to Ben and Ellie. 'We should do as he says.'

Ben felt his heart grow large and heavy in his chest at the thought of leaving the brave minotaur. Ellie ran quickly forward and planted a kiss on the bull-headed man's ugly snout. 'Thank you,' she said. 'I'll never forget you.'

Then another onslaught came from the giantess and her helpers, and the minotaur turned back to his task.

CHAPTER TWENTY-FOUR

Nemesis

Down the corridors they fled, in darkness save for the bobbing lights of the few fire-fairies which darted ahead of them. Down through twists and turns they ran, down passageways and stairs, and once down a dead end when Iggy thought he knew better than the fire-fairies which way to go. Darius's hooves thundered upon the stonework, echoing so much it sounded as if a whole herd of centaurs was careering through the castle; but despite all the noise, Ben could hear his blood pulsing in his ears and his heart thumping, and he could see from Ellie's paleness that she was just as scared as him. He wasn't looking forward to the prospect of crossing the lake again; but if it came to a choice between that and facing the Dodman and all his hordes . . .

Down the final set of steps they dashed, with Darius shouting for the selkies to get ready for a quick getaway. But when at last they reached the cavern, it was silent and empty.

Ben stared around. The selkies were nowhere to be seen. 'Skerry?' he called, and listened as his voice bounced off the dripping walls. 'Silver?'

But there was no reply.

Darius frowned. 'This is most unlike Skerry,' he said. 'However much he is concerned for his daughter, I'm sure he would never willingly abandon us.'

Ellie stamped over to the pool and stared in, her lower lip stuck out belligerently. 'Charming,' she said. 'Going off and leaving us here to fend for ourselves.' She turned to her little brother. 'Well, summon them, then,' she said impatiently. 'Go on, stupid!'

Ben felt like retorting that it hadn't been *him* who had stumbled into the Secret Country and ended up locked in one of the Dodman's dungeons, but he bit it back and applied himself to remembering the selkie's true name.

'Er, He Who Hangs Around on the Great South Rock to Attract Females!' he called a little nervously, for he found Silver's father just a bit intimidating.

Nothing.

'She Who Follows the Silver Path of the Moon?'

They waited in silence. And waited. And waited, but even Silver did not answer his call. Now Ben was beginning to feel anxiety gnaw at him. Where could they be? And how would they get out of here without them? Something must have happened – something terrible . . .

Ellie put her hands on her hips. 'Some friends they are!' she huffed. 'They've just swum off to save their skins. They're probably having a lovely time playing in the surf on some beach on the other side of the world by now!'

'There must be a good reason,' Iggy said, rubbing his head on Ben's leg for comfort. 'They wouldn't be able to resist a summons unless something had happened to them which prevented them from coming.'

'And,' said Ben, 'if anything *has* happened to them it'll be your fault – since everyone's here trying to save you, after you so stupidly got caught by the Dodman!'

Ellie had the grace to look chastened. 'So what do we do? I can swim – quite well, in fact; but this top will get ruined . . .'

Ben regarded her scathingly. 'We're a very long way underwater and I nearly drowned getting here.'

Ellie laughed. 'You always were rubbish at swimming—'

Darius waved his arms in the air. 'Stop, stop! Arguing won't get us anywhere. I wonder . . .' He waded into the shallows and stared out into the darkness. Then he turned back, a determined expression on his handsome face. 'Princess Eleanor,' he said, 'if you will do me the honour of climbing on my back, I will do my best to swim with you across the lake, and then I will come back for Ben and Iggy.' He regarded her expectantly.

But Ellie was staring at something behind him and paying no attention at all to what he was saying.

Something huge was rising out of the pool, displacing water in great sheets as it rose. Its skin was mottled and shiny. It had a beak for a mouth and two vast black eyes, one on either side of what must be its head – though it was hard to tell where its head ended and its body began. It waved some of its arms in the air. There were a lot of them, almost too many to count, and they were long and snakey and covered in suckers like horrid red mouths and fronds which looked suspiciously like fingers. In three of these vile tentacles, it clutched something greedily. But it still had a lot of unoccupied arms, and these were writhing up through the shallows in a questing sort of way.

Ben stared at it in horror. This must be the monster Silver had been afraid of encountering as they crossed the lake. The nautilus. Just like the one in one of his favourite books, which crushed ships and carried them to the bottom of the ocean.

'Look out, Darius!' he cried, too late.

As the centaur turned to confront the nautilus, two huge tentacles whipped through the air towards him. Darius reared up and beat down at the monster with his hooves, but the tentacles evaded him, snaking around as fast as thought – until one gripped him by the neck and the other by a foreleg. For a moment centaur and nautilus stayed poised in a desperate struggle; then the monster tightened its grip on Darius, and with immense and terrifying strength lifted him right out of the churning water and hurled him through the air. He struck the rocks at the back of the cavern with a resounding crash, and lay still.

Ellie screamed. Then she ran to the centaur and knelt at his side, tears streaming down her face. Tentatively, she placed her hands on Darius's powerful neck and started prodding around. How did you check a centaur's pulse? No one had ever taught her *that* in First Aid class. After a moment she looked back to Ben.

'I think he's still alive but it's hard to tell . . .'

Her tears had made what was left of her mascara run in black streaks down her cheeks, but for once Ben didn't feel like teasing her about it.

He nodded grimly, then returned his revolted gaze to the nautilus's occupied arms. For the thing trapped in the tentacle nearest to him was the old mermaid, Melusine. Her eyes were closed, and her great silver tail hung limp and dull. It didn't look as if there was any life left in her at all. 'Oh, Mellie,' Ben whispered. She'd been pretty scary herself in her time, but now she looked as helpless and unthreatening as a dead fish. He turned his eyes to the second of the nautilus's victims, and gasped. As the air of the cavern began to dry the monster's prey, it was turning from a seal into a man.

It was Skerry.

Ben felt his heart thud: for now he knew, with an awful sick feeling in the pit of his stomach, what it was that the nautilus must be clutching in its third occupied arm.

Sure enough, as the water evaporated on the third still figure, he watched in horror as sleek grey flesh turned to pale-pink skin and folds of white fabric, and silver-gold hair flowed out across the suckered tentacle – and even though it confirmed his worst fears, he could not help the loud wail of dismay that escaped him.

'Oh, Silver!'

And at once fear and horror turned to sheer fury.

'Let them go!' he roared at the beast, but it merely sent two of its tentacles out toward him, and he had jump backwards out of its way. 'As Prince of Eidolon, I command you! Nautilus, let them go!'

For a heartbeat it looked as if the monster might comply, for it hesitated and its waving arms became still. Then it opened its strange beak of a mouth and an earsplitting sound – half-shriek, half-moan – filled the cavern. And it began to squeeze the life out of its victims.

Silver's eyes shot open and she cried out in terror, a cry which ended in a wheeze as the nautilus crushed all the remaining air out of her lungs.

Ben flung himself into the water. He ran at the monster and fastened himself to the tentacle holding his friend, battering his fists against it with all his might. 'Let her go!' he yelled. 'LET HER GO!'

By way of response, the nautilus merely whipped another of its arms in his direction. Ben ducked, stepping smartly sideways. His feet went out from under him on the weed-covered steps. Down he went, fast as a sinking stone. Water rushed into his mouth and nose. He coughed and spluttered, and more went in. He tried to stand up, but a tentacle snaked around his ankles and pulled him deeper. Twisting and scraping, he kicked out, got free, shoved himself away, choking and half-blind. The nautilus's arms came after him. Water tumbled about him, solid and bullying, as much an enemy as the monster itself. Ben tumbled over and over, his lungs burning, hit first by a tentacle, then by another. It was like being trapped in a revolving door. He grabbed at something blindly . . . and it grabbed him back.

For a moment, Ben thought that was the end of it for him; that he would die here, held prisoner by the nautilus under the water until he drowned and went limp and became food. But as he felt the fight go out of him and the turmoil in the water began to clear, he realised that the thing which had hold of him was not a tentacle after all, but a flipper: a huge flipper. A vast, whiskery, tusked face was close to his own, and he realised it was Skerry – not Skerry the man, but Skerry in his true selkie form: a vast elephant-seal of a beast with huge black liquid eyes and whiskers everywhere. His mouth moved; then his eyes closed once more.

Nemesis.

Ben heard the sound as an echo in the cave of his skull. It did not sound much like Skerry, but lighter and younger and rather more human. Something else followed, but before he could think about it, his feet found something solid under them and he kicked off it as hard as he could, just as he had been taught in swimming classes. Seconds later his head broke the surface of the pool. Air rushed into his poor deprived lungs. He swallowed it down, then opened his mouth, took a deep breath, and lost it in a *whoosh* as a tentacle wrapped itself around him and started squeezing hard.

Some of the water which Ben had swallowed now shot out

241

of his mouth in a great spout, just like water coming out of the mouths of the stone lions in the fountains in Aldstane Park. He almost laughed; then something shot past his ear – something which hissed and spat and yowled horrifically.

Some other monster must have joined the fray, just when he thought it couldn't get any worse. He twisted feebly in the nautilus's grasp to see what on Eidolon it could be.

It was Ignatius Sorvo Coromandel.

The little cat had become a crazed mass of talons and teeth. His amber eyes blazed like fires. He had attached himself to the tentacle which held Ben, with every one of his sharp little claws firmly embedded in the creature's flesh, and was biting and growling and hissing all at the same time. The nautilus's grip on Ben diminished a fraction as it tried to shake the furry demon off it, but Iggy wasn't letting go.

'Give up!' he yowled indistinctly between bites. 'Release my friend Ben or you will die, you great big fat overgrown octopus!'

Unsurprisingly, this seemed to have little effect.

Now another voice added to the hubbub. Someone was talking softly in a singsong sort of voice, and the nautilus stopped its squeezing and thrashing and stilled, as if to listen. Then it started to sway, as if it were dancing. It waved its tentacles around its head, brandishing its victims, and all the little fingers on its tentacles waved as well, as if in rhythm with an unheard song. For a moment, Ben could see nothing but water as the tentacle which held him dipped down to the pool; then he was up in the air, looking down on his sister from a great height.

'You really are a huge and ugly great octopussy thing, aren't you?' Ellie crooned, the flattering smile she gave the nautilus entirely at odds with her words. 'Really, quite the most hideous creature I've ever seen, and that's saying something considering the state of Mrs McIntosh's vile poodle, Maurice, at Number Four.'

As if delighted by these insults, the nautilus swayed closer to the speaker and its hold on Ben slackened.

Ellie batted her eyelids at the beast.

'There, there, lovely monster, nice monster, good boy . . .'

Now it was above her, the fingers on its four free tentacles waving like the fronds of some gigantic sea anenome.

Ben braced himself, felt the nautilus's tentacle twitch as if in response to his tiny movement, then hurled himself free and fell feet-first on to the hard stone floor of the cavern. Miraculously, the monster made no attempt to pick him up again as he rolled and fetched up alongside his sister, panting just as loudly as Mrs McIntosh's smelly dog.

Ignatius Sorvo Coromandel landed neatly next to him, his fur sticking out all over him like a punk cat all spiked with gel.

'Wow! How did you manage that?' Ben looked back at the nautilus, and saw how its horrid eyes had grown heavy-lidded with great crescents of yellowish horn. Ellie seemed to have entranced it. Perhaps it liked being insulted by girls in clown make-up.

Ellie raised her eyebrows. 'Oh, it was just something the minotaur told me,' she said enigmatically. 'Something from a prophecy. I thought I'd try it out, since nothing else seemed to be working. Now you owe me your life.' And she gave Ben her nastiest elder-sister grin.

Ben frowned. He couldn't remember the prophecy saying anything about Ellie being able to tame monsters of the deep. She must be making it up, as usual. He gave her a hard stare, but she just returned it coolly.

'Poor Silver,' she said. 'I think he's squeezing her to death.'

Ben spun around to face the nautilus. Indeed, his selkie friend hung as limp as Mellie in the tentacles; and even her huge father seemed to be barely breathing. Ben felt his heart stop, then thunder urgently against his ribs.

'Nemesis, Lord of the Deep, release your prey!'

Ben had no idea where these words had come from: they seemed to leap out of his mouth of their own accord.

The mighty creature became as still as stone. Then it dropped the mermaid and the two selkies with a great splash into the pool.

'Xarkanadûshak!'

On the lake shore, the dragon's head came up sharply, like a dog hearing a whistle beyond the range of human ears. His wings began to unfurl.

'No!' he protested. 'Oh, no!'

'Zark, what's the matter?' The Queen was gazing at him in alarm.

'I have been summoned!' Zark's purple eyes whirled in panic. His haunches bunched themselves for take-off.

Queen Isadora placed a hand on his trembling shoulder, but

it would take more than that light touch to keep him on the ground. 'By Ben?' she cried in sudden fear, but a moment later the dragon was unable to help himself. He soared into the air, his snout pointed directly, unwillingly, towards the castle, as if someone had attached an invisible wire between him and the distant battlements.

'By my son?' she cried again in anguish.

'I am sorry, my lady!' he called back. 'He calls me against my will. I . . .'

But whatever else he said tumbled away into the rush of air displaced by his great wings and, moments later, it was with sinking hearts that Isadora and the Lord of the Wildwood saw their most loyal ally, under the spell of the Dodman's summons, setting down at their enemy's side.

CHAPTER TWENTY-FIVE

Escape

'She's dead.'

Ellie pronounced this with horror, then burst into tears. She had never actually seen a dead person before, especially not one with a long silver fish-tail.

'Poor Mellie.' Ben knelt beside her and slowly closed the old mermaid's staring eyes. There would be no more nip-chase for Melusine; no more bad singing; no more dragging of unfortunate goblins into her deep lairs for supper.

Behind him, Skerry was coughing like an old man with a bad tobacco habit, and Silver was pounding him on the back with flippers which were slowly turning to hands. Water gushed out of his mouth with every hit.

'Honestly, Dad,' she kept saying, 'every selkie knows to keep its mouth shut underwater.'

'I was . . . *cough* . . . *cough* . . . trying to warn Ben . . . *cough!*'

Silver rolled her eyes. 'Underwater, honestly.' She laughed, then clutched her ribs. '*Ow!*'

'Warn me of what?' Ben asked Skerry.

The big selkie looked surprised. 'Well, the monster, of course.'

'I thought you told me its name.'

Now Skerry looked puzzled. 'I don't know its name,' he admitted. 'I didn't even believe it existed, despite what Silver said.'

Ben frowned. So where had the name come from, then? This was all very curious.

Silver turned to Ellie. 'I hope you can swim better than your brother,' she said, 'because I'm not sure I'm going to be able to carry you all the way.'

'A brick could swim better than Ben,' Ellie grinned between sobs.

'Thanks,' said Ben. 'Thanks a lot.'

'I will carry the Princess Eleanor.'

The voice came from the back of the cavern. Ellie whirled around, to find the centaur hobbling to his feet, pale and a bit dazed, and with a rather nasty cut on the side of his head.

'Oh, Darius! Thank goodness!'

The centaur laughed, then winced. 'Just about. Alive enough, anyway, to offer my services, my Princess.'

Ellie beamed, and completely forgot to blush.

*

Zark reared away from the dog-headed man in loathing. Little wisps of smoke trickled from his nostrils. If the summoner was not protected by the magic of the summoning, he would have barbecued the Dodman on the spot.

'What do you want from me?' he demanded. 'I'm telling you now I won't do anything to harm Eleanor: I'd die first . . .'

The Dodman laughed unpleasantly. Then he reached inside his jacket, drew out a brace of struggling fairies and bit their heads off. He closed his eyes, sucked hard on their severed necks and savoured the taste of their magic. When he opened his eyes again they were bright red, as if lit by some inner fire. 'You will do whatever I wish of you, dragon, and then you may die. Quite horribly, if I have my way. And of course I shall. I always do. But there's really no need to toast the little Princess. Yet. Come with me.'

Compelled by the magic and sickened by the wanton destruction of the innocent creatures, Zark followed the Dodman down the stairs, his wings grazing painfully against the walls on either side. Whatever else it had been built for, the castle had not been designed to contain dragons with any degree of comfort. Hounds and goblins squealed and fled at the sight of him, shoving past, getting underfoot, scrambling over each other to get away. No one liked dragons much: they had heard too many tales of roastings, and Boggart had been nastily burned by this particular specimen once before. Besides, fire in such close quarters was a worrying prospect, even at the best of times, let alone with the lord of the castle in such a bad mood, and a minotaur on the loose only a few steps away . . .

'Burn that door down!' the Dodman boomed as they reached the bottom of the stairs.

Grizelda, who was still leaning her considerable backside against said door, slowly began to look alarmed. 'Hold on—!' she began, but Zark's chest was already swelling up with combustible gases.

The first mighty blast burnt most of the giantess's hair and eyebrows off, and left a smouldering hole in the oak door the size of a goblin's fist. An eye blinked – once, twice – on the other side of the hole, then vanished.

'Again!' cried the Dodman.

Zark opened his mouth a second time.

At this point, Grizelda wailed and pushed past him, shedding bits of charred clothing as she lumbered up the stairs, her hobnailed boots ringing on the stonework like hammers on an anvil.

Now the centre of the door succumbed to the blast, falling away into charcoal and ashes. The minotaur and the Dodman regarded one another steadily through the smoke.

Then, with a huge bellow, the minotaur charged at the remains of the door, wresting the blackened timbers from the frame, and hurling them at the Dodman and his cohorts. In the chaos that ensued, the minotaur turned and disappeared into the warren of tunnels below.

'I will take Ben,' Skerry said, 'if you can manage the Wanderer?'

Silver nodded. 'Just watch your claws, little cat, eh? I saw the damage you did to the nautilus!'

Iggy grinned proudly and polished his claws on his coat.

'What do we do about this thing, though?' said Ben, staring gloomily at the pool, then at the nautilus, which was still lurking with its strange black eyes just above the surface, watching him, unblinking, its arms all hanging limply underwater. It was very unnerving.

'It seems to be enspelled,' Darius said. He looked at Ben with a new respect. 'Did you Name it, by any chance?'

'Yes,' said Ben hesitantly. 'And then Ellie sort of sang to it.' Recent events were all jumbled up in his mind: he wasn't sure about anything any more.

'It seems to have decided to do your bidding,' the centaur told him. 'Which is probably just as well—'

At that moment, an almighty hullabaloo broke out. Bellowing, snorting, wailing, howling, screeching, gnashing, yowling, shrieking noises filled the air. Up there in the dungeons, the door which had separated the Dodman and his creatures and their friend must have been opened.

Ellie looked distressed. 'What about the minotaur?' she had just started to say, when the bull-headed man came crashing down the stairs.

'The Dodman is coming, and he has a dragon!' he cried, charging across the cavern. He skidded to a halt at the edge of the pool, his fiery eyes bulging. 'What on Eidolon is that?'

'There's no time to explain. We have to get out of here!' Darius said, as calmly as he could manage. 'Can you swim?'

'With these horns? I'd sink like a stone.'

Ben and Darius exchanged looks. Then they both looked at the nautilus.

'It's the only way,' the centaur said.

'I don't know if it'll do what I ask it,' Ben replied quietly.

'We don't have a choice.'

'Go,' the minotaur said. 'Don't worry about me: I just came to warn you and make sure you got away. I'll hold them off while you make your escape.'

'No,' said Ben. 'We're not leaving you. Nemesis, Lord of the Deep, will you please carry my friend, the minotaur, across the lake to the safety of the Wildwood shore, and then go back to where you came from and do no harm to any of our friends?'

The minotaur eyed the nautilus uncertainly. 'Me, go with that thing? I'd rather take on the Dodman.' But he didn't sound entirely sure of that either. And a second later, he didn't have the choice. The next thing he knew, two of the nautilus's vast tentacles were securely wrapped around his torso and he found himself suddenly clutched to the monster's glutinous body.

'Take a deep breath!' yelled Ben, and then the nautilus and its passenger were gone in a great vortex of churning water.

Ellie made a face. 'I'm so glad I'm coming with you,' she told the centaur, hugging his neck.

Scuffling footsteps sounded on the stairs leading down to the cavern, accompanied by yelpings and the chattering of angry goblins.

'Ben!'

The voice was familiar, even through the echoey corridors.

Ben frowned. 'Zark!'

'Get away, Ben!'

And then there came the sound of a dragon in pain, and the howl of a maddened dog.

'No time to waste: come on!' Darius plunged into the pool, Ellie holding on for dear life.

'See you on the shore,' Silver said to Ben. 'Just remember not to open your mouth underwater this time, okay?' And she winked at him, tucked Iggy securely under one arm and dived smoothly into the pool.

Ben cast one despairing look over his shoulder as the corridor behind them lit up with the red of dragon fire, and then he just had time to remember to take a very deep breath as Skerry leapt in.

I hate this, Ben thought as the water closed over his head, forcing itself all over him like a great cold glove. He closed his eyes. Perhaps if he really concentrated this time he could hold his breath without passing out. He felt the body of the selkie under him transforming from human to seal, the friction of skin giving way to sleek slipperiness; and he gripped as hard as he could with his knees and arms.

CHAPTER TWENTY-SIX

Pursuit

The Dodman aimed a booted foot at Zark's belly. 'You stumbled on purpose, dragon! To hold us up and allow your little friends to get away!' Then he let fly.

Zark felt the kick break one of his ribs, but he wouldn't give the dog-headed man the satisfaction of seeing his pain. Instead, he drew back his long muzzle and growled, being careful to show all his curving ivory teeth. How he wished he could bite the Dodman in two . . .

'Back!' The dog-headed man waved his arms furiously at the jumble of goblins and hounds which had tumbled down the steps once Zark had unblocked them. 'Get back up to the courtyard! Boggart! Beetle! Get the chariot, and Grizelda; and some knives! Harness up the hounds and the wolves. We are not finished here yet. And you –' he bent his face close to Zark's whirling purple eyes '– you will come with me, *dragon*.'

'What is that? Look, over there: breaking the surface of the lake . . .'

Something had emerged from the depths and was heading at speed in their direction. No: not some*thing*, but a number of them. The grey waters rippled with activity as these shapes cleared the shadow cast by the castle's tall walls.

The Lord of the Wildwood shaded his eyes. 'I cannot quite make it out . . .'

Now everyone was staring out at the lake, their eyes squinting against the bright morning light. Two of the Wildwood fairies soared into the air to get a better look.

'I can see Darius!' one of them cried. 'And he's got a girl with him!'

'It must be Ellie!' Isadora's hands flew to her face. Her green eyes shone wildly.

'And there are two selkies, too. One of them's got a boy with it; and the other's clutching something too, but I can't quite see what it is.'

'A boy?' The Queen went even paler than she had been before. 'Are you quite sure?'

'Yes, yes!' the fairies chorused.

Cernunnos stared out at the scene, his face darkening. Then

he nodded grimly. 'It's Ben,' he said, and his antlers rattled as he spoke. 'Though how he came to be here, Eidolon only knows.'

Isadora stood on tiptoe, trying to see her children better. 'Come along, my dears,' she breathed, not sure whether to be relieved or terrified.

A moment later, there came the unmistakable sound of the Wild Hunt belling and calling, and a spectral procession launched itself off the battlements: a dozen ghost-hounds, yipping and slavering, followed by six white wolves drawing a chariot full of goblins brandishing wicked-looking curved blades, and a huge dark, ragged figure. Behind them, a dragon sailed into the morning air, described a graceful circle and then plummeted down towards the disrupted surface of the water.

'Oh, Zark!' cried the Queen. 'Oh, no!'

On the dragon's back, gripping tight to its crest with its hands and to its wide-bellied body with its spiky knees, was a single tall figure, every line of its body and its sharp-nosed head taut with murderous intent . . .

'Look out!'

Ellie ducked as Zark's outstretched claws whizzed past her, catching a strand of her hair and tearing it away.

'Ow!'

'Blasted dragon, you missed on purpose!' The Dodman struck out with his boot as the dragon banked, catching the centaur a glancing blow.

Darius, his face grey with exhaustion, rolled sideways, almost dumping Eleanor in the water.

The dragon wheeled overhead, its wings beating the air fiercely.

'Zark, Zark: what are you doing?' Ben shouted. 'It's us. Why are you doing this?'

'He's been summoned. He's acting under an unbreakable compulsion,' Skerry said. 'He can't help it. As far as I can see, he's doing what he can to avoid hurting anyone, but the Dodman's not going to let him get away with that for long. And here comes the Wild Hunt! Take a deep breath, Ben, we're going under again!'

Ben just had time to see the leading Gabriel Hounds inches above him before the water closed over his head. This time he'd forgotten to fill his lungs, and moments later his lungs were bursting. He held his breath as long as he could, then dug his knees sharply into the selkie. Skerry bucked and twisted, then shot to the surface.

Ben had time to take a single deep breath before the Wild Hunt was upon them. A goblin slashed at him with its sharp little knife, and Ben had the wit to flatten himself against the selkie's slick skin, before grabbing Gutty by the wrist. With a sudden jerk, he'd pulled the goblin out of the chariot.

At once, three of its fellows had Gutty by the ankles, not really trying to save him, but more to claw their way closer to Ben. Whoever captured one of the Queen's children would get a big reward: their master had promised them.

Skerry made a sharp turn so that Ben lost his hold on the goblin, but he managed to grab the curved blade – and then they were underwater again and barrelling along. When Ben opened his eyes, he could see Silver in front of them with Iggy plastered to her side like a wet rag. Iggy had his eyes screwed tightly shut. He obviously wasn't enjoying himself at all. Ben almost smiled; but a moment later he could see Darius, his legs kicking feebly, and the water churning around him.

This time when they surfaced, it was to a cacophony of noise: Ellie screaming, goblins chattering, wolves howling, and hounds barking like banshees. Two goblins had hold of Ellie and were slowly dragging her from the centaur's back, while Darius was reaching around in vain behind him trying to hold her on.

'Help me!' Ellie shrieked. 'Ben, help me!'

One of the goblins twisted its claws in her hair and yanked her head back. 'Did he say he wanted her alive?' it asked Bosko.

Bosko shrugged. 'He's so furious he won't care!'

Batface leant out of the chariot and swiped at her with his curved knife; but Ben launched himself off Skerry's back with the stolen blade in his hand, and the two weapons clashed with a screech which shivered through the air – and Batface overbalanced and fell into the lake. Ben fell with him. Down they went, tangled up in one another, with Batface trying all the time to bite and stab. Ben twisted in the goblin's grip and kicked away from it, and then he was free of it and swimming in dark water, a long way out of his depth.

It took a moment to realise this; and then he panicked. At the swimming baths he had mainly swum widths in the shallow end, since he was, as Ellie had said, about as talented at swimming as a brick. Once, he'd tried lengths, but as soon as he passed into the deep zone and knew he could no longer touch the bottom, he'd got nervous and all his muscles had gone leaden. Luckily, he'd been on the outside lane and could grab the bar; but there were no bars here with which to pull himself out. He felt his legs going heavy, and then he started to sink. He dropped the knife and kicked out wildly, but to no avail; then he was underwater and going down . . .

'Ishtar!'

The Queen called three times; on the third call a tiny dark speck appeared in the sky overhead and grew larger and larger with every passing second.

'I have returned your mate and kit,' the female dragon said, as she came in to land. 'Just as you asked me to.' She sounded very annoyed.

'I am sorry to summon you,' Isadora said breathlessly, 'but I need your help. The Dodman . . .' Helplessly, she indicated the battle taking place on the lake.

'That's Zark!' Ishtar gaped, craning her neck. Her eyes bulged in disbelief. 'What's he thinking of, carrying the Dodman around like that?'

'The Dodman summoned him,' Cernunnos said.

'And how did the Dog-Headed One know my husband's true name?' Izzy asked sharply.

No one answered her. Instead, the Queen started to clamber on to Ishtar's back.

'What do you think you are doing?' the Horned Man demanded, clutching at her arm.

'I have to do something,' Isadora answered fiercely, unpicking his fingers. She managed to get a leg up on to the dragon's withers, and swung herself up to sit astride its neck. 'Since no one else is doing anything. Ishtar, as one mother to another, I implore you: help me save my children!'

The great blue-and-purple-and-gold dragon craned her neck around at the Queen, then nodded her assent. She reared up, beat her long wings so hard that the Lord of the Wildwood had to stand aside, and took off.

Staying high above the lake, Ishtar planed like a gull on a current of warm air, and the Queen of Eidolon peered down anxiously. She could see Ellie astride the centaur, and a selkie with a small dark cat stuck to it; she could see the Gabriel Hounds and the white wolves which had once belonged to Cernunnos himself, drawing a chariot full of goblins and a very strange-looking figure in charred clothing with a soot-covered face and bald patches. But nowhere could she see Ben, or, for that matter, the Dodman.

'*Ishtarrr!*'

Ishtar sideslipped swiftly, and not a moment too soon. Zark barrelled past, neck outstretched and wings stiff and uncoordinated as if he was willing his body not to obey the compulsion the Dodman had placed upon him. The dog-headed man, known in another world as Mr Dodds, leered at the Queen over his shoulder.

'Ready to give yourself up to me, are you, my dear? You didn't need to arrange your own transport, you know.'

Isadora gritted her teeth. 'You're a monster!' she cried.

261

'Ah yes, they do say that.' Now the Dodman had steered Zark into flying a parallel course to Ishtar. 'Personally, I think monsters have had a bad press, often from nuisances like your own very dear husband. Him, I will deal with next. Oh, and the baby, of course. Once I've cleared away your family in this world.' And he gave her his shark's grin.

'Where's my son?'

'Oh, drowned by now, I'd say. We saw him go down some time ago. And sadly there was nothing we could do to help him. Now –' and here a growl slipped out '– are you going to come quietly, or am I going to have to kill the worm you fly upon and take you by force?'

'Never!' cried Isadora. 'Down, Ishtar, down!'

Zark's mate folded her wings back like a stooping hawk and plummeted towards the lake.

Grizelda never saw what hit her. Ishtar's talons raked out left and right, and over went the chariot – goblins, giantess and all – into the lake. The traces got all tangled up with the wolves, who then started taking out their frustrations on the hounds harnessed in front of them. Soon, the entire Wild Hunt was fighting with itself.

Ishtar skimmed past at speed and was gone before a single creature could lay a tooth or claw upon her.

'There!' cried Isadora. 'Over there!'

She indicated a struggling figure a little way ahead of them. It was the centaur, battling valiantly on through the water towards the shore, though the last of his strength was waning. On his back, weighing him down, was not only Isadora's daughter, Eleanor, but also three of the Dodman's goblins, squabbling over her. Beside them, Silver and Iggy were trying to help; but flippers and a small cat's fury were no match for three determined goblins armed to the teeth and greedy for reward.

Cernunnos and his phalanx of centaurs were wading out into the lake, but they would never reach them in time.

Yawing sharply, Ishtar made a low pass across the surface of the lake and grabbed two of the goblins in her talons. They squawked in horror as she tossed them aside and went in for the third. The last goblin, a mangled bandage flapping around its head, wrapped its arms and legs around Ellie and refused to budge. It had already lost an ear because of this scrawny little human, and it didn't want to lose anything else to the Dodman's rage.

Ishtar roared, and grabbed both girl and goblin up in her claws.

With the goblin obscuring her vision, Ellie had no idea what was going on. One minute she had been fighting for her life, the next she was in the air in some monster's grasp. She screamed and screamed.

'It's all right, Ellie,' her mother cried through the din. 'We've got you now, you're safe.'

But Isadora spoke too soon.

Xarkanadûshak hurtled into his wife, howling all the way, compelled by the Dodman's will. In a great flurry of limbs and wings, both dragons crashed into the surface of the lake.

Vast plumes of water erupted into the air, as if the entire

lake was trying to empty itself upwards and change places with the sky. Everyone stopped what they were doing, transfixed by the shocking noise of it all. The Lord of the Wildwood stared into the confusion, searching desperately. Then he urged his centaurs forward.

'Find the Queen!'

Not many folk from either world know much about dragons. Stories abound, mainly of violence and treachery, of greed and arrogance. They are known for their destruction: for the breathing of fire and the eating of sheep and maidens. Amongst dragonkind, however, there are other stories: tales of courage and selflessness, tales of heroism and sacrifice.

When the Dodman gave Xarkanadûshak the order to attack his wife, there was nothing Zark could do but obey. But he did so shrieking a warning as he came; and although the collision appeared terrible to the onlookers, Ishtar moved fast, and it was a glancing blow he struck his wife, which sent Izzy and the Queen spinning harmlessly out of his way. Zark, however, carried on. Headlong he dived into the lake, dizzyingly fast, before the Dodman could make him do anything else. Down and down he went, driven by a compulsion all his own.

It is worth it! he told himself fiercely, over and over. *If I can rid the world of the fiend on my back, my wife and kids will lead safer lives, and so will the rest of Eidolon. My life is a small price to pay. My life . . .*

He tried not to think about that bit. A second later he felt

264

the Dodman trying hard to take control again, digging his horrid dog-nails into the sensitive places between his scales, biting and kicking.

For Eidolon, Zark thought to himself. *For Eidolon and my friends and loved ones.* And he shut his mind to the Dodman and watched the lake-bed come looming closer and closer.

He had often wondered how his death would come to him. When the dog-headed man had captured him and sold him to the woman in the Other World he had thought it would be there, tied to a fencepost by a piece of frayed string amongst dead leaves and piles of rubbish he didn't understand, feeling his magic and his life leaking out of him moment by moment into the bad air. No one would even have known – had Ben not saved him. Now it was his turn to repay that deed. No one made songs for dragons who died a quiet death tied to a fence-post far from home; at least this way he would live on in heroic tales.

He folded his wings as tightly as a furled umbrella, closed his eyes and waited for the inevitable impact.

It never came.

The next thing Zark knew, he was flying through the water at a speed he could never have dreamt possible, and something had him firmly by the midriff, something which squeezed him with monstrous strength. Beneath the grip, he could feel the Dodman squirming, furious but feeble against this overwhelming force, and Zark could not help but crane his neck in curiosity. He felt the water bashing at the back of his head in their headlong rush. But when he stared around, it was not into the dead black pupils of the dog-headed one that he found him-self looking, but a pair of mismatched eyes, one a sensible hazel-brown, the other a vivid Eidolon green.

It was Ben, and he was gripped in the snakelike arms of the same monster which grasped Zark and the Dodman. He should have been terrified, but instead he was smiling as hard as he pos-sibly could with his mouth held tightly shut to keep the lake out of it. Then he tapped the great mottled arm which held him three times and pointed upwards, and suddenly there was a great *whoosh* as the monster – a vast nebulous shadow beneath them – gathered itself and drove them up towards the light with phenomenal power.

They burst into the bright air seconds later, held aloft by the tentacles so that water streamed from them in sparkling rainbows.

Ben coughed and coughed; then he laughed and laughed. 'Thank you, Nemesis!' he said. 'That was brilliant!' His eyes were shining as he turned to Zark. 'He saved me, you know, even though he's really scary. I was drowning again, and he dropped the minotaur in the shallows and came after me.'

The dragon blinked. Nemesis? Drowning? Minotaur? It was all too much to take in.

'And then we saw you crash into Ishtar and Mum, and it looked really bad, so we came to see what we could do, but when we got there Mum and Izzie were fine and Mum had got hold of Ellie, and so we came after you, because it looked as if you were going too fast to stop and I was really worried you were going to hit the bottom!' Ben finished in a great rush.

Zark didn't know what to say. He looked at his friend, and then he looked away.

A shadow passed before Ben's mismatched eyes. 'You were . . .' he breathed. 'You were going to . . .'

The dragon nodded. 'I could not kill him directly; but I thought if I hit the lake-bed hard enough and rolled, I would die there and trap him beneath me. And in time, and with luck, he would drown, and the world would be rid of him.'

Ben regarded him solemnly. 'That was really brave, Zark. But I couldn't let you do it. What would Izzy do? What about your kits?'

The purple eyes whirled and whirled. 'Someone has to stop him.'

Benjamin Arnold firmed his jaw. 'Yes,' he said. 'That's true. Someone has to stop him.'

He tapped the giant squid on its tentacle again, and its fringe of fingers flexed and swayed in response.

'Nemesis: will you please take me and the dragon to the shore and release us there; but keep a tight hold of the dog-headed one known as the Dodman. Do you understand me?'

The nautilus quivered and a weird chirrup emerged from its beak of a mouth.

Ben looked at Zark. 'I do hope that means yes.'

Two strange and motley groups had gathered on the southern shore of Corbenic Lake. On one side, away from the forest, was a sodden giantess, a pile of wet goblins and some very miserable-looking hounds. A black bird with a bright-orange beak flapped around overhead, shrieking. Only the words 'Dodman' and 'cowards' and 'guts for garters' could be made out at a distance.

On the other side were a herd of centaurs with their manes and tails dripping puddles on to the stones, and six white wolves who had broken free of their traces and were now licking the remains of the lake and the taint of the Dodman off their fur. There were two dragons, one of scarlet-and-gold, the other of purple-and-blue, preening like eagles caught in a rainstorm; and two selkies, one big and one small, transforming moment by moment into a man and a pretty fair-haired girl. There was a pale woman in a soaking dress with her arm around a shivering girl in a pink T-shirt. Both were being wrapped in a cloak of moss and leaves by a tall figure with the branching antlers of a stag. Next to them there was a boy with straw-blond hair and mismatched eyes, who was squeezing water out of his jumper and grinning from ear to ear. A small black-and-brown cat sat at his feet, rubbing its bedraggled head against his leg over and over and over. And at the back of the group, in the shadows cast by the forest eaves, a vast figure with a massive bull's head and a pair of menacing horns watched over the scene with eyes of fire, but a remarkably benign expression for one who owned such a fearsome and bloodthirsty reputation.

A sudden scream of outrage made everyone stop whatever they were doing and crane their necks for a better view.

Out in the deepest part of the lake, with Corbenic Castle rising behind it like a great golden mountain, a giant squid was wrestling a tall dog-headed figure into submission. The Dodman – held high in the air by a vast tentacle – was struggling valiantly: sinking his claws and teeth into the huge, rubbery arm; biting at the suckers and fingery things; kicking and squirming and cursing between grunts and growls and howls. It had been a bitter discovery to the Dodman that Naming the squid had absolutely no effect: for the Lord of the Deep was still safely under the compulsion placed upon it by Ben Arnold, Prince of Eidolon. And so the dog-headed man was taking out his frustration on the nautilus itself, who barely felt a thing. In its turn, Nemesis turned one of its huge black eyes upon its captive and regarded it with whatever degree of humour a giant squid possesses. Then it began to squeeze the Dodman just a little harder, and a little harder – until the dog-headed man stopped trying to harm it and hung there, helpless and panting, planning terrible revenge on everyone and everything in sight.

Ben picked up the little cat and cradled it against his chest.

'I'll never eat fish fingers again,' he vowed solemnly.

'Fish don't have fingers.'

The voice was soft and trilling, like the breaking of waves on a sandy beach. He turned around to find Silver smiling at him, all girl now, her pale-gold hair glowing in the sunlight.

'You do!' Ben said, grinning from ear to ear.

'I am *not* a fish.'

'You are sometimes. Sort of.'

'And you are a horrid boy.'

Ignatius Sorvo Coromandel turned to regard the selkie with

his sardonic amber eyes. 'That's not what you said before,' he reminded her wickedly. 'When you thought he had drowned.'

She Who Swims the Silver Path of the Moon looked away. 'I don't know what you mean,' she said, flustered.

Ben looked at her. Then he looked at Iggy. 'What are you on about?'

'Silver knows.'

By now, Silver was blushing furiously. 'Shut up,' she said to the little cat.

'What'll you give me,' Iggy wheedled, 'not to tell him? Will you bring me goldfish and silverfish and copperfish?'

'Yes!' said the selkie desperately.

'And catfish and dogfish and rabbitfish?'

'Yes!'

'And some of those fat little crabs from the beaches off Doubting Sound?'

'Yes, yes!'

'Goodness me,' growled Ignatius Sorvo Coromandel, dropping Ben a great big wink. 'She really doesn't want you to know how much she cares.' And then he had to scamper off as fast as his paws could carry him, because when selkies have feet instead of flippers, they can move as quickly as any cat.

Epilogue

In the throne room of Dodman Castle an angry figure paced up and down, muttering to itself and glaring at anyone or anything that got in its way. No one dared say a word. Especially the word 'nautilus' . . .

Nemesis had held on to its prize for long after the compulsion of Ben's Naming had worn off. The goblins had watched from the shore with macabre fascination, wondering whether or not the giant squid would finally squeeze the dog-headed one to death, and squabbling over who would dare to swim the lake and retrieve the keys to the castle's extensive larders.

But eventually the nautilus had grown bored, or decided it

had something better to do, and after setting the Dodman down on the rocks below the castle (none too gently), it had dived down into the deepest part of the lake. No one had seen tooth nor tentacle of it since.

It was with considerable circumspection that the Sphynx entered the throne room, knowing all too well the Dodman's likely state of mind. He had lost his hostage (and a rather dangerous minotaur in the adjacent cell), and he had almost had the Queen in his grasp, before losing her too. But worst of all he had lost his dignity. There were a lot of creatures spreading the tale across Eidolon of how a boy – believed to be the son of the long-lost Queen of Eidolon – had thwarted the mighty Dodman; of how the dog-headed one had hung, powerless, pathetic and dripping, in the grip of a giant squid commanded by the young Prince.

None of this would have improved the Dodman's already bad temper.

The spy skirted the groups of sullen goblins (since the lost battle, they had been on reduced rations as a punishment for their failure), avoided the tethered Gabriel Hounds – who watched him pass with hungry eyes and frothing jaws – and came to a halt at a safe distance from the pacing figure.

'Ahem,' it said, and got ready to run beneath the throne in case one of those nailed boots which scraped and squeaked on the stones suddenly came its way.

The Dodman turned slowly.

His eyes – usually so fierce and shiny black – were dull and rimmed with red. It looked as if he had not slept in a week (which, in fact, he had not). He barely glanced at the hairless cat and continued his distracted pacing.

'What do you want with me, little sneak? Have you come to tell me how they snigger behind my back? How they flock to Isadora's cause now that they fear me no longer? How the Queen prides herself on my defeat?'

'Of coursssse not, master—'

'Because it is not a defeat. NOT, do you hear me? It is a . . . a . . . temporary setback, that is all.'

'Yesssss, master. I came with newssss that may brighten your day.'

The Dodman stopped in mid-stride, turned and regarded the Sphynx with renewed interest.

'It will take a great deal to brighten the gloom that has settled over me, little spy.'

'If you would accompany me to the battlementsssss, ssssire . . .'

Now the Dodman's eyes narrowed with suspicion. He surveyed the throne room to see if there was anything going on – but the goblins were as cowed and craven-looking as usual, and the giantess was snoring in a heap by the fire, on top of several squashed hounds. Was there a plot afoot, a plot to maybe tip him over the castle walls into the waters of the deep lake below? He shuddered. Ideas like this had been plaguing him by day and night; and being worse by night, he had ceased sleeping for fear that someone, somewhere, was hatching something to cause his downfall, now that they were less afraid of him than they had been.

'Why to the battlements, spy?'

'You will see, sssire. Sssomeone has a gift for you.'

A gift.

As he followed the Sphynx up the winding stairs to the top of the castle, the Dodman ran through all the possibilities in his head. None of them seemed either likely or welcome; and when he reached the battlements, his spirits were not raised by the sight of a dark speck circling high up in the clear blue sky above him.

The weather in Eidolon had improved of late. Ever since the Queen had returned: more so since she had secured her daughter and retired to the safety of the Wildwood to fortify the resistance against him. It was yet another thorn in his side. Wicked deeds required foul weather: thunder and lightning, sweeping storms, driving rain – to quell the hopes of the small folk and make them seek the shelter he and only he could provide within these walls.

He squinted against the bright sunlight, shaded his eyes with a dark dog-nailed hand, and watched as the speck got larger and larger.

It was a thin, spiky figure with bright-orange hair, all knees and elbows as it fought to control a classic willow-wood broomstick in the stiff updraught above the castle. A large parcel was balanced precariously in its lap.

'Ah,' he said at last. 'I see it is the little witch. Bad day, Cynthia.' He inclined his great dog's head.

'Bad day, Dodman.' And Awful Cousin Cynthia, known by her true name in the Shadow World as Cynthia Lucrezia Creepie, gave the dog-headed man her most awful grin. Despite the existence in the Other World of plenty of good dentists and effective whitening toothpastes, it was a truly ghastly grin, full of slimy green-and-black teeth and too much gum. 'I have something for you.' She paused. 'Though if I give it to you, you will have to promise me something in return.'

The Dodman looked thoughtful. 'Tell me first what the Queen and her vile brood are up to.'

Cynthia looked annoyed. She ran an impatient hand through her carroty hair. 'Ben and Ellie have gone back to the Other World to rejoin their father and the horrid baby. And to go back to school. Ha! Such a waste of time. And the Wanderer has gone with them.' She laughed. 'A useless bodyguard he'll be! Even my Sphynx could beat him.'

The Sphynx looked uncomfortable at this idea. Amongst cats, tales circulated that Iggy had fought valiantly at Ben Arnold's side, taking on a huge, tentacled monster single-pawedly, and later killing several goblins. However, since there had been no other cats present to witness these heroic events, he suspected these stories had probably originated with the Wanderer himself . . .

'And the Queen?'

Cynthia shrugged. 'With the Lord of the Wildwood, gathering her forces. There's word that she will try to persuade the dragons to her cause, but they are refusing their support so far.'

The Dodman looked hang-dog. 'Dragons,' he groaned. Even the walls of Corbenic Castle would not withstand the onslaught of dragons. 'If she Names them, I am lost.'

Cynthia's horrid grin widened. 'Perhaps not. She refuses to compel them; and now she cannot!'

'Cannot?'

Cynthia unwrapped the parcel in her lap and held it up to his view, just out of reach.

The Dodman's eyes grew round with wonder. 'The Book! The Book of Naming! Give it to me!' He fairly danced on the spot. 'Oh, with the Book of Naming I can bring the dragons to my cause – even better, I can Name the dinosaurs! Imagine the Wildwood trampled to matchwood beneath the feet of a herd of brontosauruses! Imagine the centaurs devoured by tyrannosaurus rexes! Imagine the Queen carried off by a pteranodons and brought to her wedding flanked by velociraptors!'

'Stop!' cried Cynthia. Beneath the Book, something else glittered. She fetched it out and set it on her head, where it rocked dangerously on her narrow skull. It was the Crown of Eidolon. 'If you want the Book, you will have to make me a promise.' She paused. 'Actually, two promises.'

'What?' He might have known there was a catch.

'First of all, you are to rescue my father from jail and return him safely to the Secret Country. And secondly, once we have dealt with Isadora and her brats, you shall bow to me as your rightful Queen!'

The Dodman regarded her askance. He'd been planning to spring Aleister from prison anyway: but it wouldn't do to look as if he was giving in to the little witch's demands too easily. 'Well, now, that's a lot to ask.' He stroked his hairy dog-chin thoughtfully. The second part of the bargain would be a lot more difficult to keep . . .

'Promise me now, or lose the Book forever.'

Cynthia hovered before him, and the sun glinted on the crown, almost blinding him with its brightness.

The Dodman crossed his fingers behind his back and gave her his finest smile. The sun of Eidolon gleamed on each and every one of his powerful dog's teeth.

'It is my pleasure, my dear, to make these promises to one as beautiful as you. Now, give me the Book and we can peruse it together in the comfort of my throne room.'

Cousin Cynthia giggled and went all pink with delight.

It clashed horribly with her hair.

THE SECRET COUNTRY
BY JANE JOHNSON

JANE JOHNSON

The Secret Country

"Full of the kind of magic a child longs for... you'll never see your cat in the same light again!" BRIAN PATTEN

Ben has been saving for weeks to buy the Mongolian fighting fish he's seen in the local pet shop. But on entering the Pet Emporium, a small cat hooks his claws into Ben's jumper and begs to be bought and saved from Mr Dodds, the pet shop's cruel owner.

The cat, Iggy, has an amazing story to tell. He comes from a place called Eidolon, or the Secret Country, which exists as a shadow-world to our own. It is a world filled with magic, and mythical creatures like dragons, selkies, sprites and centaurs.

Ben and Iggy must travel between the worlds to help the magical creatures return home. On their journey Ben will make loyal friends, encounter great danger and discover his own royal lineage in the mysterious Secret Country...

ISBN: 0-689-86080-3